Naguib Mantouz

Morning and Evening Talk

Naguib Mahfouz was one of the most prominent
writers of Arabic fiction in the twentieth century.
He was born in 1911 in Cairo and began writing
at the age of seventeen. His first novel was published in 1939. Throughout his career, he wrote
nearly forty novel-length works and hundreds of
short stories. In 1988 Mr. Mahfouz was awarded
the Nobel Prize in Literature. He died in 2006.

THE FOLLOWING TITLES BY NAGUIB MAHFOUZ
ARE ALSO PUBLISHED BY ANCHOR BOOKS:

The Beggar, The Thief and the Dogs, Autumn Quail
(omnibus edition)
Respected Sir, Wedding Song, The Search
(omnibus edition)
The Beginning and the End
The Time and the Place and Other Stories
Midaq Alley
The Journey of Ibn Fattouma
Miramar
Adrift on the Nile
The Harafish
Arabian Nights and Days
Children of the Alley
Echoes of an Autobiography
The Day the Leader Was Killed
Akhenaten, Dweller in Truth
Voices from the Other World
Khufu's Wisdom
Rhadopis of Nubia
Thebes at War
Seventh Heaven
The Thief and the Dogs
Karnak Café

The Cairo Trilogy
Palace Walk
Palace of Desire
Sugar Street

Morning and Evening Talk

Morning and Evening Talk

A NOVEL

Naguib Mahfouz

*Translated from the Arabic
by Christina Phillips*

ANCHOR BOOKS
A DIVISION OF RANDOM HOUSE, INC.
NEW YORK

FIRST ANCHOR BOOKS EDITION, MARCH 2009

Copyright © 2007 by Naguib Mahfouz
First published in Arabic in 1987 as *Hadith al-sabah wa-l-masa'*
English translation copyright © 2007 by Christina Phillips

The Cataloging-in-Publication Data is on file at
the Library of Congress.

Anchor ISBN: 978-0-307-45506-2

www.anchorbooks.com

Printed in the United States of America
10 9 8 7 6 5 4 3 2

Note on the Arabic Alphabet

Morning and Evening Talk is made up of a series of character sketches in Arabic alphabetical order according to the first name of the title character. The complete alphabet is as below, with the name of each letter transliterated in English.

أ	Alif	ر	Ra'	ف	Fa'
ب	Ba'	ز	Za'	ق	Qaf
ت	Ta'	س	Sin	ك	Kaf
ث	Tha'	ش	Shin	ل	Lam
ج	Gim	ص	Ṣad	م	Mim
ح	Ḥa'	ض	Ḍad	ن	Nun
خ	Kha'	ط	Ṭa'	ﻫ	Ha'
د	Dal	ظ	Ẓa'	و	Waw
ذ	Dhal	ع	'Ayn	ي	Ya'
		غ	Ghayn		

Morning and
Evening Talk

Alif

Ahmad Muhammad Ibrahim

THE SKY WAS A CLEAR BLUE, the shadows of walnut trees slumbered on the ground, and the surface of the old square shone in the sunlight and clamored with endless noise from the surrounding alleys. Bare feet, ornamental slippers, pantofles, and the hooves of horses, donkeys, and mules trampled over Bayt al-Qadi Square, where the new police station met the old courthouse. Ahmad emerged into this vast playground and quickly forgot the house he came from, his parents' house in Watawit. He was four years old when he was brought to his maternal grandfather's house on Bayt al-Qadi Square to relieve the loneliness of his uncle Qasim, who was a year and a half older than him. With the other sons and daughters married, the house was empty; no one was left except the father, Amr Effendi, the mother, Radia, and their youngest child, Qasim. Qasim only knew his sisters, Sadriya, Matariya, Samira, and Habiba, and brothers, Amer and Hamid, as fleeting guests of his parents and would visit them in the same manner he would visit the branches of the family living on Khayrat Square and in Suq al-Zalat and East Abbasiya. At his sister Matariya's house in Watawit he liked her son Ahmad best. Ahmad had an older brother called Shazli and a baby sister, Amana, but Ahmad was by far his favorite. Matariya loved Qasim like a son so let

Ahmad go and live with his grandparents and relieve Qasim's loneliness in the big empty house. Muhammad Effendi Ibrahim, Ahmad's father, did not like the idea and nor did his mother, Aunt Matariya, but they let him go, determined to reclaim him the moment he was old enough to attend Qur'an school. Qasim knew nothing of their hidden plan and delighted in the company with unadulterated happiness.

Ahmad was a paragon of beauty. He had a rosy complexion, blue eyes, soft hair, and a winning personality. He would follow his uncle about the square like a shadow. The two of them watched the snake charmers, watering carts, and policemen filing by. They met Amm Karim the ice-cream seller together and observed funeral processions with a sense of dread. Women from the neighborhood would gaze at Ahmad as they passed.

"Who's this handsome lad?" one would ask.

"Ahmad, Aunt Matariya's son," Qasim would reply proudly.

"The handsome son of a beautiful lady," she would say and go on her way.

"Don't fill Ahmad's head with tales of ifrit," Muhammad Effendi Ibrahim used to chide Qasim's mother, Radia. She regarded him with contempt and replied, "What an ignorant teacher you are!" The man laughed, revealing his overlapping front teeth, and continued smoking his pipe. This was because it was usually Radia who put the two boys to bed. Elation would fill their hearts as they listened to her fairy tales before going to sleep, as the miracles of saints and the mischief of ifrit flooded their imaginations and reality submerged in a world of dreams, marvels, and divine signs. In their spare time she took them around different houses and the tombs of the saints and the Prophet's family. The fun and entertainment continued until one day Qasim was taken off to begin a new life at Qur'an school and Ahmad was denied his friendship for two-thirds of the day. The Qur'an school was situated a few steps from the house in a recess in the Kababgi Building, but it was surrounded by a fence of strict tradition that turned it into a prison where divine principles were learned under threat of the cane. It was no place for entreaties and tears. Qasim would leave in the afternoon and find Ahmad and Umm Kamil waiting for him at the gate. The world was not the same anymore; inescapable worries had crept in. His instincts told him Muhammad Ibrahim, Ahmad's father, posed a further danger for he did not like living apart from his son. His bulging eyes began to regard him coldly.

"I don't like that man," he said to his mother.

Her long brown face darkened. "How ungrateful you are! Didn't he send you his son?" she said.

"But he wants him back."

She laughed. "Do you want him to give up what is his for your sake?"

One day Ahmad was not waiting for him when he left the Qur'an school. Instead, he found his mother looking more grave than usual.

"Your friend is sick," she said.

He found Ahmad in a deep sleep in his bed. His mother prepared vinegar compresses, muttering, "Dear boy, you're scorching like a fire."

She recited verses from the Qur'an nonstop. When Amr Effendi came home in the evening he decided to send Umm Kamil to notify Matariya and her husband. When the incense and incantations did not succeed in bringing the fever down, Amr Effendi fetched the neighborhood doctor, but he said he was only an eye doctor and recommended they send for Doctor Abd al-Latif who lived in Bab al-Sha'riya.

"But he is married to the belly dancer Bamba Kashar!" Amr protested.

The doctor laughed. "Bamba Kashar doesn't mean he can't be a good doctor, Amr Effendi."

The doctor married to the famous belly dancer arrived. Qasim could feel the tension in the air. He heard his mother say, "I don't trust doctors. I recognize only one doctor—the Creator of heaven and earth."

Days went by. Where was Ahmad? Qasim wondered. Where had his freshness and beauty gone?

One afternoon he returned from Qur'an school and met a new scene at home. His family sat in a strange silence. His mother and Ahmad's grandmother were in Ahmad's room and his brothers and sisters—Amer, Hamid, Sadriya, Samira, and Habiba—were in the living room. Matariya was sobbing and Muhammad Ibrahim was next to her, smoking his pipe despondently. His heart was infused with fear at the somber atmosphere. He realized that the enemy he had heard about on formal occasions in the past, that he had seen reigning over funeral processions heading toward al-Hussein, had somehow invaded his house and snatched away the person he loved most in the world. He screamed and cried until Umm Kamil carried him up to the top of the house. Through the summer room jalousie he saw Ahmad's grandmother, with an embroidered bundle in her arms, board a carriage with her daughter and Amr Effendi. The carriage moved off, followed by a second carrying Amer, Hamid, and Qasim's uncle, Surur Effendi—a funeral procession of a new kind. Was this the end of Ahmad? He refused to believe or accept it. He was convinced they would bring him back that day, sweet and rosy once more. But he still could not stop crying. In the evening everyone dispersed.

"That's enough!" his father chastised.

"Where did you take him?" he asked expectantly.

"You're not a child anymore," said Amr. "You attend the Qur'an school and learn suras from the Qur'an by heart. Ahmad has died. Everyone dies according to God's decree. It's the will of God."

"But why?" he protested.

"The will of God. Don't you understand?"

"No, Papa."

"Stop. . . . This is no way to behave before God. Ahmad will go straight to paradise, which is a wonderful destiny. Be careful not to misbehave."

"I'm very sad, Papa!" he shouted.

"Recite the opening sura and your heart will be soothed."

But his heart was not soothed. He wept whenever he thought of Ahmad and it was said he was even sadder than Ahmad's mother. He did not recover from his grief until his world fell to pieces and a new creature no one had predicted was born.

Ahmad Ata al-Murakibi

A giant among men, tall and broad, the contours of his face might have been found on a statue. His blood coursed vigorously under his tan, and his thick mustache, outspread palm, and hirsute hands made him the image of a hero of popular legend. He would fill the whole seat of the carriage as it sauntered through Bayt al-Qadi Square and came to a halt in front of the old house when he visited in the halo of a great feudal lord. He would receive his nephew Amr Effendi—who was the same age—with a heartfelt embrace and greet Radia warmly, then set his presents down on the console, asking, "Where's Qasim?" His voice was calm and soft, which was peculiar considering the colossal body it came from, and in his brown eyes shone a languid, friendly look furnished with kindness and peace, as though he were a huge mosque where glory and security unite. "Tell us, how are our children?" he would say, referring to Amr and Radia's sons and daughters. He visited everyone in the family periodically, in particular the daughters, so as to reinforce their standing before their husbands. He heaped candy on Qasim and was saddened by Ahmad's death, whom he had been very fond of, for he was such a handsome boy.

He would usually stay for dinner, on the condition that Radia serve one of the traditional Egyptian dishes for which she was famous alongside pre-prepared ta'miya and kebab side dishes, then spend the evening with Amr and his brother, Surur, at the Misri Club. The poor branch of the family was happy when rich relatives, like the Murakibis and the Dawuds, came to visit and reveled in the lasting effect it had in the quarter, although Radia would nevertheless remark to Amr, "None of them have roots. They all come from the soil," then turn to Qasim and carry on provocatively, "One man vanquishes them all and that's your grandfather, Shaykh Mu'awiya." Amr would smile and remain silent, preferring peace.

Yet Qasim never got over the magic of the Murakibi mansion on Khayrat Square. As big as Bayt al-Qadi Square and as tall as the Citadel, it had a garden like a zoo, countless rooms, and nothing could match its furniture; what wonderful antiques of all shapes and sizes, and bronze and plaster statues in the corners! The wives of Ahmad Bey and Mahmud Bey, Fawziya Hanem and Nazli Hanem, had amazing complexions and blue eyes. Here was a real-life world even more magical than the world of fairy tales and dreams. Qasim's grandmother, Ni'ma Ata al-Murakibi, was the sister of Ahmad Bey and Mahmud Bey, but she was poor and had nothing in the world but her two sons, Amr and Surur, and daughter, Rashwana. Nevertheless, the two wealthy brothers loved their sister and her children, especially Amr Effendi, who was marked by natural wisdom. Ahmad Bey strengthened his ties with Dawud's family, the relatives of his sister Ni'ma's children, and other relatives through marriage—despite the mutual jealousy between the rich branches—and would invite them to the mansion on Khayrat Square. Abd al-Azim Pasha Dawud preferred Ahmad to his brother, Mahmud, as he was gentle-natured, straightforward, and modest, but when the Murakibi family was mentioned at Amr's house he would nevertheless declare scornfully, "They're even more ignorant than they are rich. Where do they come from? A poor pantofle seller in Salihiya!"

While Mahmud Ata would say of Dawud's family, "Resounding titles but they're mere hirelings at the end of the day!"

"We're all children of Adam and Eve," Ahmad would say in his usual pious way.

Amr, Surur, Mahmud, and Ahmad started school around the same time and made do with the primary school certificate. Amr and Surur entered the civil service because they were poor, and Mahmud plunged into life's tribulations under his father's wing, but Ahmad gravitated to calm and a life of luxury so was discounted from his father's plans. He spent some time on the farm in Beni Suef on the margins of farming then returned alone, or rather with Fawziya Hanem, to his rooms on the third floor of the mansion in Cairo. He spent his time visiting family and receiving friends. His magnificent drawing room was made up to receive friends and relatives. They would sip tea, coffee, and cinnamon, play backgammon and chess, send for lunch and dinner, and stay up until dawn during Ramadan and on festivals. The phonograph was his companion when he was alone, the carriage his recreation, Shubra and al-Qubba Gardens his visiting spots, and al-Sayyida his place of worship on a Friday. Some nights he attended Sufi gatherings with his cousin Amr, who was a member of the Dimirdashiya order.

When his father, Ata al-Murakibi, died, his tranquil evergreen life suffered a violent blow that shook him thoroughly. He was suddenly faced with a huge responsibility he was not equipped to deal with: managing the land left to him—three hundred feddans, not to mention the additional hundred or so from his wife.

"You'll learn everything," said Mahmud Bey. "There are people to help you. But," the man clenched his hulking hand into a fist and continued, "you'll need to give up your amicable ways. You can't treat peasants and tenants as you do friends and relatives."

Ahmad thought for a long time, groping about the snare, then said, "You're my older brother. I've known only kindness and loyalty from you. I wasn't made for this."

Thus, Mahmud took his father's place. Fawziya Hanem was unimpressed with the decision. "You decided too quickly and didn't consult anyone," she said politely.

"Do you doubt my brother?" he asked, confused.

"He may be your brother but why grant him trusteeship?" she said in good faith.

"He's my brother and dear friend and you're his wife's sister. Our family is a model of harmony and affection. I did what I thought was right," he said.

His comfortable life continued and he received his share of the profits without inspecting it; everything was fine and he had no worries. Then the 1919 Revolution pounced and shook him profoundly. He was ignited by the leader's charm and, at his brother's suggestion, donated ten thousand Egyptian pounds to the cause. They followed their father's old exhortation of maintaining a distance from politics and avoiding anything that might arouse the anger of legal, or any other, authorities: the tide is too strong to swim against. But when discord between Sa'd and his opponent, Adli, began to emerge and the party split, the men deliberated about what to do; or, rather, Mahmud reflected and Ahmad went along with him.

"The time for sentimentality is over. It's time to be smart," said Mahmud.

"The whole nation is behind Sa'd," said Ahmad.

"We should go where our interests are best served."

Ahmad paid attention.

"Don't be taken in by the rhetoric," Mahmud went on. "The English are the real power. Adli is close to them but he won't bring security forever. The power with a permanent channel to the English is the Crown. Let's pledge allegiance to the king."

"You're right as always, brother," said Ahmad with resignation.

Their stance was soon known in Bayt al-Qadi, where Amr and Surur lived next door to one another.

"It's inappropriate," Amr muttered with characteristic calm.

"These rich relatives of ours, God has given them immeasurable wealth and unequaled depravity," Surur scorned.

Amr had more than one reason to refrain from berating them; on the one hand his peaceable nature, on the other the marriages of his sons Hamid and Amer to Shakira and Iffat, the daughters of Mahmud Bey and Abd al-Azim Pasha. Nevertheless, he let his thoughts be known to his uncle Ahmad Bey when he had dinner with him at the mansion.

"God knows I'm with you in heart. It was Mahmud's decision," Ahmad said smiling.

"Every day the square below the house seethes with demonstrations. The shouting for the destruction of the traitors fills the air," said Amr with regret.

"People with interests don't like revolutions, cousin," replied Ahmad.

It was Ahmad who bore the brunt of the criticism since he was with people day and night whereas Mahmud spent most of his time steeped in business on the farm. The announcement of allegiance during those difficult times earned the brothers the rank of pasha on the festival of the coronation, bringing both men immense pleasure. Ahmad gave a banquet and invited everyone—men and women alike—from Amr, Surur, and Dawud's families. The mansion was decorated as if for a wedding. Ahmad immersed himself in his private life up to the top of his head and did not let the nation's worries infiltrate his solitude and sully it. However, as time passed and his children grew up, he encountered trouble from unexpected quarters. His eldest son opposed his decision to place himself under the trusteeship of his brother and entered into a long and obstinate dispute with his mother to start with, then his father. He pestered his father until he promised to reclaim the property he had renounced entirely of his own accord. The spark ignited a fire, which blazed in every corner of the close-knit family. Ahmad seized the opportunity when Mahmud next visited Cairo on business. He raised the subject timidly and concluded the speech with an apology, "The children have grown up. They have their own ideas." Mahmud mulled over what he had heard for a while, seething with anger. He was marked by unlimited power. At the mansion his family enjoyed more prestige than his kind, meek brother's. Fawziya Hanem feared him and complied with his orders while she debated with her husband as an equal. Ahmad's two sons were decorous and obedient in his presence but affectionate, exuberant, and casual in front of their father. The reins were slipping out of his hands.

"You're weak! How can you allow your son to behave like this?" Mahmud demanded.

Ahmad was hurt but did not want to lose his children's respect. "There's no need to speak cruelly, brother," he said.

"Do you doubt my good care?" Mahmud asked brutally.

"God forbid," he said hurriedly. "But I'm entitled to take charge of my own affairs."

"So you're entitled to ruin yourself at your idiotic children's instigation?"

Ahmad frowned. "I seek refuge in God."

There followed a discussion with Ahmad's eldest son, Adnan, which Mahmud Bey regarded as an unacceptable impertinence. The young man addressed his uncle with a bluntness the elder found offensive. The fire spread. The two brothers quarreled, each wife rallied to her husband's side, ripping their sisterly loyalty apart, and the nieces and nephews traded the worst insults. The family bond was lacerated. Each branch withdrew to its own floor of the mansion, as though they did not know one another. The efforts Rashwana, Amr, and Surur expended to repair the rift failed and Amr's son Hamid, who lived with his wife, Shakira, on Mahmud Bey's floor, found himself torn and hard-pressed to maintain good relations with his great-uncle Ahmad's family. Ahmad Bey moved to the farm in Beni Suef to assume management of his land in old age. He cultivated what was his to cultivate and leased what was his to lease. It brought him troubles he had not foreseen and losses he had not anticipated. Shortly before the Second World War, he developed hemiplegia and was taken to his bed in Cairo to wait for the end. He was the first of the second generation to fall; various illnesses would soon call the rest to join him in some way or other. Amr was still healthy and went to visit Mahmud Bey and said, "It's time to forget the quarrel and its reasons and return to your brother."

Mahmud was silent, pensive. "The matter will never be forgotten but I will do what is appropriate. . . . "

Ahmad's family knew only that Mahmud Bey sought permission to enter the room. They gathered and stood for him courteously with tears in their eyes. His wife and children were with him. When the handshaking was over he announced, "The rift is over and forgotten. My heart beats as kin."

He approached his brother, who was lying prostrate on his bed, silent and motionless. Fawziya leaned over his ear and whispered, "Your brother, Mahmud Bey, has come to reassure you."

Mahmud leaned over him, kissed his cheek then stood up and said, "Forgiveness is God's. Take heart."

Ahmad lifted his heavy eyelids. It was clear he was trying to speak but could not get any words out, though no one doubted his flushed cheeks were quivering with goodwill. He passed away in the middle of that sad night.

Adham Hazim Surur

He graduated as an architect in 1978. He entered working life aged twenty-five in a Cairo awash with troubles, yet never encountered a single problem in his own life. Torrents of people and vehicles surged around him, the noise erupting like the rumble of a volcano, yet he lived happily at his parents' villa in Dokki in peace and tranquillity amid the scent of roses and flowers. While his generation fumbled about, searching for identity, a home, marriage, and selfhood, he found an important position awaiting him at his father's engineering office. He was good looking like his father and similarly shortsighted, almost blind, in his left eye. He cared for nothing in the world except his chosen field and knew only dreams of fortune and success. So mild was his faith he had almost none, without being an atheist.

"We lost his older brother. Let me arrange his marriage!" Samiha Hanem, his mother, said to his father, Hazim.

"This generation makes its own choices. Don't provoke him," the man replied gently, careful as always not to anger her. But she flared up as usual.

"There's a rotten root in your family and I'm frightened it'll lead him down the same path as his brother," she shouted.

His father lit a cigarette. "Do what you think is right."

But Adham was much quicker than she imagined and informed them one morning during the holidays, as they sat in Mena House Garden, that he had chosen his life partner. Samiha was alarmed. She stared into his face questioningly. The young man guessed her fears and smiled. "Karima. She is in her final year of law school. Her father is Muhammad Fawzi, a government legal advisor."

His mother's nerves appeared to relax. She put a spoon of ice cream between her wrinkled lips and began chewing.

"Inquiries will have to be made," she mumbled.

Adham frowned.

"It's just the formalities. I'm optimistic," his father said obligingly.

Visits were exchanged and the choice met with approval, though some critical comments on Samiha's part were inevitable.

"The mother is evidently not educated," she said to her husband.

The man was amazed at her remark since she—Samiha—had not herself obtained the baccalaureate, but he said only, "It's not important."

Everything was agreed on. Hazim bought his son an apartment in al-Ma'adi for six thousand Egyptian pounds and Adham moved there with his bride at the end of the year.

Of his family tree Adham knew only his mother's branch; his grandfather, Muhammad Salama, who set up the engineering office, and his maternal aunts and uncles. As for his father's side, he knew vaguely that his grandfather, Surur Effendi Aziz, was employed in the railways, that his great uncle, Amr Effendi, worked at the ministry of education, and that he had paternal aunts with children, but he never saw any of them. He also knew his family came from al-Hussein, a quarter he associated with poverty and backwardness, but there was no reason to remember it and he only ever passed through in a car. He often encountered members of his family in squares and public places without him recognizing them or them recognizing him. His father followed his movements with pleasure, confident that when he retired one day in the not too distant future the office would be left in capable hands. He once said to him with respect to the corruption that was rife, "There is plenty of opportunity out there. You have knowledge, intelligence, and ambition. Don't digress. Don't scorn advice. If you mock values then at least strive for a good reputation and beware of jail."

Amana Muhammad Ibrahim

She had a radiant complexion, delicate features, soft hair, and was the image of her mother, Matariya, but for two front teeth that stuck out a little. She was Matariya's last child, born a few months before Ahmad's death. Her uncle Qasim was fond of her, but dared not claim her as he had her deceased brother; he loved her from a distance until his personal tragedy wrenched him away from worldly concerns altogether. Her paternal grandmother died when she was seven and she mourned her more than was warranted for someone of her age. She entered primary school without opposition thanks to the times and, likewise, went on to secondary school. Matariya was only interested in marriage but said to her husband, "Like my sister Samira's daughters, everyone wants an education these days." Muhammad Ibrahim accepted this without discussion. He had been promoted to a senior teaching post by staying at the Umm Ghulam School through the good offices of Abd al-Azim Pasha Dawud.

As it happened, Amana displayed a promising propensity for learning and her talent for mathematics was clear. University seemed an easily attainable dream. She passed the baccalaureate, but in the summer holiday that followed, her father developed a galloping illness and he soon died, while only in his fifties. The family inherited the house, his pension, and the rent from the shop below the house. The Second World War was by then over and from the second generation Amr, Surur, and Mahmud Ata had passed away. Thus, Matariya felt she was facing life alone. During this period, Abd al-Rahman Effendi Amin, an employee at Dar al-Kutub, requested Amana's hand. He was fifteen years older than her and had a good reputation. Amana liked him but wanted to finish her education first.

"Our circumstances mean marriage comes first," Matariya said with sympathy. She consulted her mother, Radia, who said,

"A suitable man is a thousand times more important than university." She looked at Amana admiringly. "Why would a girl of your beauty be interested in education?"

Her uncle, Shaykh Qasim, said to her, "I saw you in a dream dancing in the district of Gamaliya!"

Matariya asked her mother what the dream meant and she said without hesitation, "The district represents peace and security, the marital home. . . ."

Matariya provided Amana's dowry, the value of her and her paternal grandmother's jewelry, and what little was left of her late husband's savings. Amana was wedded to her groom on Azhar Street.

It was evident that love sheltered the new couple in its wing, but from the beginning harmony between husband and wife required stubborn efforts. Abd al-Rahman Amin believed in the man's authority, while Amana was extremely sensitive, fussing over an ant's nip like it was a snakebite. She was quick to burst into tears and shut herself away or head off to Watawit from Azhar Street. Matariya would escort her back and try and resolve the mess, then end up embroiled in the quarrel herself. Her older sister Sadriya said to her, "Your daughter's husband is no worse than mine but no one gets to know what goes on between us. Don't interfere in their private affairs and don't side with Amana in every disagreement."

Radia learned of the newfound bickering and sought refuge in incantations, spells, and tomb visits. The dissension constantly threatened to escalate until the specter of divorce raised its ugly face like a bat. The extent of the problem was compounded by the fact that the moment Amana gave birth to her first child, Muhammad, and was overwhelmed with motherhood, the beautiful wife all but disappeared. After him, she gave birth to Amr, Surur, and Hadiya and the specter of divorce withdrew, although the bickering continued and constant stress left its mark on her face.

The children started school with the first generation of the July Revolution. They departed the gloomy atmosphere of the house and hovered in skies of fortune and splendor before drowning in the sea of confusion that swallowed its victims on June 5, 1967. They began their working lives after the demise of the first leader, and during the wave of victory and the infitah policy they were awarded contracts to work in other Arab countries. Even Hadiya did not stay behind. As for Matariya, she died after suffering many disappointments: the premature deaths of her youngest son and husband, the aberrations of Shazli, and Amana's bad luck. Abd al-Rahman Amin eventually succumbed to old age. Amana savored her children's success, though old age and illness overtook her too before her time. She saw her respected uncles and aunts and the rest of her relatives pass away. She read the book of sorrows as it turned its pages one after the other and would listen to the prophecies sent down to Shaykh Qasim and try to apply the verdicts to her destiny.

Amir Surur Aziz

He was born and grew up in Bayt al-Qadi. Surur Effendi's house was next door to his brother, Amr Effendi's, and Amir was around the same age as his cousin Qasim. He played and roamed about with his cousin but was kept away from him after his tragedy. Unlike his brothers, he was strong bodied, inclined to be overweight, and loved fun. In terms of chivalry and piety, he most resembled his uncle Amr. He knew the 1919 Revolution as a legend of demonstrations, battles, and anecdotes and grew up a faithful and patriotic Sa'dist. He tried to mimic his brother Labib's accomplishment and industry and made successful progress, though he never reached his brother's level. His piety and spirit of decorum and tradition were a detriment to relations with his sister, Gamila, who was four years his senior, for he objected to what he saw as casual behavior unworthy of the family name and honorable religion. No one in his family shared his views. They became increasingly annoyed with him until his father said, "You're too zealous. Leave the matter to me."

In secondary school he began participating in the party struggle that broke out after Sa'd Zaghloul's death. He joined in demonstrations protesting Muhammad Mahmud's dictatorship and spent two weeks in hospital after he was struck by a club. He had three relatives in the police with sensitive positions at the ministry of the interior; Hamid Amr, his cousin, and Hasan Mahmud Ata and Halim Abd al-Azim Dawud, his second cousins. They consulted on the matter and the one closest to him was assigned the task of cautioning him and setting him on the right path. Hamid delivered the speech in the presence of his uncle Surur and father, Amr.

"Your name is at the top of the blacklist at the Interior," he said to his cousin.

"I'm honored," Amir laughed, as he did often.

His cousin pointed to the scar on his temple and said, "You can't always rely on being so lucky."

"They won't hesitate to discharge you from college," said his father.

"I'm a Wafdist like you, but must advise you," said Hamid.

The young man did not conceal his disdain for Ata and Dawud's families. He sensed his father was not overly fond of them and scoffed at their roots at every opportunity. He began to light the political sky at the center of the young Wafdists and was the one they would proffer to the Wafd leaders. His ambitions for the nation reached for distant horizons. His brother Labib, who was a public attorney at the time, tried to put the brakes on his exuberance but he said, "I've discovered my path and won't ever turn back."

"What if you lose your job? You know we're poor," he inquired with natural calm.

"Then I'll work for the press," he replied confidently.

But he did not lose his job or work for the press or continue his political struggle. At the beginning of Ismail Sidqi's time, during the flood of demonstrations protesting against the abrogation of the 1923 Constitution, he was shot dead in Muhammad Ali Street. The security forces took charge of his burial, along with many others, so as to prevent their funeral processions from paving the way for further demonstrations; only his father, uncle, and brothers were permitted to attend. His premature death shook Surur and Amr's families profoundly. They recalled what Shaykh Qasim had said to him at the end of one visit to his uncle's house: "You will raise the red flag." They interpreted the words as a reference to the blood spilled the day he was martyred.

Ba'

Badriya Hussein Qabil

SHE WAS BORN IN AN APARTMENT in a modern block on Ibn Khaldun Street, the first child of Hussein Qabil, the antique dealer in Khan al-Khalili, and Samira, the fourth child of Amr Effendi. The quarter was fragrant with the perfume of westernized Jews and the apartment radiated elegance, good taste, and affluence. As Badriya grew, sweetness infused her features and gracefulness her manner. When she visited the old house in Bayt al-Qadi with her parents, her early maturity would attract attention. Amr Effendi, her grandfather, chuckled and said, "She'll be wearing the higab and veil before long."

"But she is going to continue until she finishes her education, Uncle," said Hussein Qabil.

"What a weird, wonderful world," Radia laughed.

"We won't treat our sons and daughters any different," said Samira.

"Even if a bridegroom comes round the corner?" asked Radia.

"He can wait or go in peace," Samira said without hesitating.

"Samira, you're quite the odd one out in this family!" said her father, disguising his objection with a smile.

When she reached adolescence a merchant on a visit to her father's shop saw her and wanted to marry her, but he turned

away when he discovered he would have to wait until she finished her education. Another visitor came forward whom they
could not satisfy. Then, in her fifteenth year, sitting on the bal-
cony with her mother and brothers and sisters, she suddenly
collapsed, her body rigid, her limbs shuddering, her mouth
foaming. Alas, it was epilepsy. Qasim's tragedy was etched in
people's hearts but this was epilepsy of the most violent kind.
The doctor was summoned and advised rest, a change of air,
and extremely gentle treatment. She stopped going to school.
The glow in her wide eyes was replaced by a vacant, dazed look,
and her ability to converse vanished, replaced by senseless jab-
ber. Samira appealed to her mother for help.

"If she could do anything she would have done it for her
son," said Hussein Qabil.

But Samira did not accept this argument so Radia came with
her incense, spells, and incantations. She took the girl around
the tombs of the saints and the Prophet's family but the situation went from bad to worse until only a ghost remained.

One morning, Badriya said to her mother, "I dreamed a
prince was summoning me to go for a walk in al-Qanatir."
Samira's heart was gripped with foreboding. Death came for the
girl at noon and she passed away. Thus, Samira lost a daughter
just as Matariya had lost a son; but Samira's had been in the
prime of youth. She was surrounded on all sides by condolers
from the families of Amr, Surur, Mahmud Bey Ata, Ahmad Bey
Ata, and Abd al-Azim Pasha Dawud. How Radia grieved. Whenever she thought about her daughter's situation she would whisper to her lord, "Have pity, O Merciful and Compassionate."

Surur Effendi secretly resented Radia. He suspected she was
the reason neither of his two daughters were chosen by any of
her sons and reviled her in his usual manner. He said to his wife,
Zaynab, "It all derives from Radia's family; all the men and
women in it are touched with madness, her first and foremost."

Baligh Mu'awiya al-Qalyubi

He was the last of Shaykh Mu'awiya al-Qalyubi's children and the brother of Amr Effendi's wife, Radia. He was born in the shaykh's house in Suq al-Zalat in Bab al-Sha'riya, the only infant born to the shaykh after his release from prison. He had a religious upbringing from the outset and his father enrolled him at al-Azhar when he was still young. When he visited his sister Radia in Bayt al-Qadi, his youthfulness, jubbah, caftan, and turban turned heads. He occasioned a mixture of reverence and merriment in her family for by nature he sated both sides, reciting the Qur'an in a fine voice at his sister's request and joking with her sons and daughters. He had an attractive, round, wheat-colored face and his love of fine cuisine was evident; he knew as much about different kinds of food as he did about the religion he studied.

"You'd be better as a cook than a theologian like your father," Radia remarked with her biting tongue.

He chuckled, "I'm wavering between a scholastic father and a sister who fraternizes with ifrit."

Around this time, Shaykh Mu'awiya departed for the land of his Lord. He arranged Radia's marriage but did not live to see the wedding. After his death there was no one to curb Baligh's impulses. One day, Radia and her old mother, Galila, were sitting on the sofa in the hallway, presided over by the stove with the well to its left. Radia could tell from her mother's somber manner that she was immersed in a sea of worry that was unusual for her. When she asked what was wrong, her mother replied, "Would you believe it, Radia? Your brother has begun coming home each night in a drunken stupor!"

"God forbid!" cried Radia, alarmed.

"I'm powerless."

Radia found herself even more powerless than her mother. She turned to Amr Effendi for help, but Baligh only feigned remorse and continued his wayward behavior. He provoked general disapproval and increasing indignation all round. Reports eventually reached the Azhar administration and the affair ended with him dismissed and disbarred before obtaining his religious diploma. He found himself lost, without a source of income. His mother owned some vacant land and ceded it to him. He sold it and decided to invest the proceeds in a wholesale grocery business. He traveled to his father's relatives in Qalyub and began purchasing cheese and butter and transporting it back to Cairo to distribute to grocers. With the outbreak of the First World War he made notable profits and his finances improved. From then on his star rose brightly. Around this time he married Amina al-Fangari, who came from a wealthy and respected family. With the Second World War his fortune reached its zenith. He erected apartment blocks and built a mansion for himself in al-Qabisi, which became known in the quarter as "The Abdin of al-Qabisi" on account of its majesty and splendor. He only produced one son, whom he envisaged as a senior judge. He proved to be a skilled merchant, yet all his life he never recovered from the malady for which he had been expelled from al-Azhar. He would visit Bayt al-Qadi from time to time in a carriage, and later a car, laden with gifts, secretly watching the impression he made with boundless pleasure. He continued to pray and fast and give alms as much as he drank and was as persistent in seeking forgiveness as he was conceited and proud. He lived to the beginning of the 1950s, after Ahmad Ata, Amr, Surur, Mahmud Ata, his mother, Galila, and sisters, Shahira and Sadiqa, had passed away, and when only his older sister Radia, the one who fraternized with ifrit, remained. He developed cirrhosis of the liver, spent half a year in his comfortable bed, and then died in his sleep—or so it appeared to his wife, Amina al-Fangari.

Bahiga Surur Aziz

The square of Bayt al-Qadi witnessed her childhood games with her brother Labib and sister Gamila. While growing up she mixed with her uncle Amr's sons and daughters. She shared the calm temperament of her older brother, Labib, and cousin Samira, and was the same age as her cousin Qasim. Her face was white and radiant like her mother Sitt Zaynab's, glowing and rosy. Her eyes were a clear green and there was in her voice a richness that recalled her father, Surur Effendi. Her natural composure meant that some mistook her as dull, whereas her respect for tradition and piety prevented her from misbehaving like other children. Like her uncle's daughters and her sister, Gamila, her education ended with Qur'an school, and, like them too, she applied herself to cooking, sewing, and other household chores and assumed her place in the customary queue for a suitable man when still very young. Her cousin Hamid was probably the most suitable one in the family, but Ata al-Murakibi's family seized him for themselves, sounding alarm bells for Surur Effendi and his wife, Zaynab Hanem. They had been through a similar experience once before when hoping to marry Gamila to Amer.

"Didn't you think of Bahiga before you gave Hamid to Mahmud al-Murakibi?" Surur asked his brother.

"We are poor men at God's door, Surur. We have to examine our birds to find their feathers! Your daughter Gamila, praise God, will not wait long," Amr replied.

Surur's feelings toward his older brother and the rest of the family thus alternated between love and bitterness. He unleashed his tongue on his relatives like a merciless dagger, which ultimately lowered his ranking in their affections below that of his brother, Amr. The futile platitudes Amr offered a second time round exasperated Zaynab. She retained her outward cool but nevertheless announced bitterly, "I know what is behind all this!"

"My brother is deeply conscious of his lowly place before our wealthy relatives," said Surur. "He is always eager to strengthen his ties with the family's richer branches."

"Don't forget either that Radia, ally of the jinn and black magic, is jealous of me and sparing with her kindness."

Bahiga was unconcerned by the loss of Hamid—she disliked his coarseness and vulgar manner anyway. At the same time, she observed with disgust the scandalous mischief her sister, Gamila, was carrying on with her cousin Qasim. Her sister was sixteen years old and her cousin was twelve, or perhaps a little over. What was it she sometimes caught them doing on the roof and under the stairs? Good morals repelled it and religion cautioned against it. But she kept it secret for fear of the consequences. Then, after Gamila was engaged to be married and had become sensible, she found it was her turn to think about Qasim. However, she was not reckless and foolish like her sister. Her heart beat with tender love, locked in a cage behind steel bars of shame and tradition. The boy noticed her and read the silent summons in her clear eyes. He complied, overflowing with desire and hoping to continue with her the games interrupted by Gamila's disappearance. He found a loving heart, but an iron will. He hovered around her like a madman until her mother declared, "You're the same age so he is not right for you."

She did not protest, but nor did she agree.

"He has a long way ahead of him. Don't forget his mother," Sitt Zaynab continued.

Bahiga felt wretched. When the young man suffered his tragedy and was presumed lost she was completely drowned in misery. She had no choice but to resume her place in the queue for a suitable man. But the wait stretched out inexplicably until tongues in the family consigned her to the same basket as her aunt Rashwana's daughter, Dananir. She was a pretty girl and a paragon of good morals so what kept the suitors away? The waiting and heartache dragged on and on until her uncle Amr, her father, Surur, and her mother, Zaynab, had all passed away.

In 1941 she was alone in the old house next door to her uncle's in Bayt al-Qadi with only the maid, Umm Sayyid. Her brother Labib's work kept him away from Cairo and he would only visit as a guest. Despair gnawed away at her night and day as she approached thirty; she had nothing in the world except a share of her father's pension. Then suddenly—as if by revelation—Shaykh Qasim awoke to her once more and said to his mother, "I want to marry Bahiga!" Radia interpreted the request as a miracle, a decree sent down from the clouds. She spoke to Labib about it the next time he visited. The man thought for a long time. His cousin was not short of money but . . . ? He put the question to his sister and met with consent. Was it despair? Was it the love from long ago? Was it fear of loneliness? The marriage the family had long joked about took place one night as Cairo suffered a major air raid and convulsed with the sound of antiaircraft fire. Bahiga moved to her uncle's house as Qasim decreed he would not leave home. Years went by, but there was no sign of children.

"You will give birth to a boy when the moon is content," Qasim assured her.

In 1945 she gave birth to a son, who his father named al-Naqshabandi. He started school after the July Revolution and drank of splendor and glory throughout his education. He was blessed with a radiant face, slender body, and shining intellect. He graduated as an engineer in 1967 and was sent on a delegation. Radia was in her final days when she said goodbye. His father said to him, "God is with you. I bid you farewell without tears." Al-Naqshabandi traveled to West Germany a few months after June 5, crestfallen and somber. He learned there of the death of the leader, but did not mourn. When he obtained his doctorate he decided against ever returning to Egypt. He worked in Germany, married a German, and took up German nationality. When his father learned of this he said once more, "God is with you. I bid you farewell without tears."

After Radia died, Qasim and Bahiga remained in the old house behind the walnut tree that had witnessed their love long ago. Their hearts still beat with love and solitude.

Gim

Galila Mursi al-Tarabishi

SHE WAS BORN A QUARTER OF THE WAY through the nineteenth century in Bab al-Sha'riya to a father who worked in a tarboosh factory that was set up, along with other factories, by Muhammad Ali. Her father was a relative of Shaykh al-Qalyubi and lived near his house in Suq al-Zalat, so he betrothed his daughter, Galila, to his neighbor's son, Shaykh Mu'awiya, who at that time was starting out as a novice teacher at al-Azhar. Thus, Galila became mistress of the old house in Suq al-Zalat and was known about the quarter as Galila al-Tarabishi. She was so tall she towered over the shaykh, for which he never forgave her. She was dark skinned, slim, had a high forehead and wide brown eyes. With the passing years, she gave birth to Radia, Shahira, Sadiqa, and Baligh. She was renowned for her encyclopedic knowledge of mysteries, miracles, and popular remedies; it was as though she had taken something from every religion from the time of the pharaohs to the Middle Ages. Shaykh Mu'awiya tried his best to teach her the principles of Islam but through their many years together he took from her more than he gave. He obeyed her when he was sick and, when a mishap befell him, would bow his head for her magic spells, surrender to her incense, and repeat incantations after her. She was stubborn and, if the need arose, aggressive, hence the neighbors were extremely careful around her. She imparted all her knowledge and experience to her daughters and they responded to her variously. Radia embraced her bequest more wholeheartedly than the others and claimed more of her love than the other children, including Baligh.

Whenever Shaykh Muʻawiya tried to assert authority over her she would defy him stubbornly; even the threat of divorce did not frighten her. He was aware of her moral strength and superior domestic skills so would back off and be content with armistice and co-partnership. She was utterly dedicated and rigid in her beliefs and this was made plain the day her husband, Shaykh Muʻawiya, died during the Occupation. The engagement of Radia and Amr had been announced according to an agreement reached between Shaykh Muʻawiya and his friend Aziz Yazid, Amr's father. An hour after his death, as Sitt Galila's cries broadcast the bad news, the bride's hamper arrived, the most important gift from the bridegroom, who did not know what had happened. Galila accepted the gift—a fish the size of her son Baligh—and gave the carrier his portion. Its arrival in the middle of the loud sobbing made her uneasy and she feared the consequences for her favorite daughter's future. She leaned over the shaykh's head, shrouded in a green wrap, and whispered from her wounded heart, "Forgive me, Muʻawiya." Then she hurried to a room on the eastern side of the house which looked out to the mosque of Sidi al-Shaʻrani in the distance, telling herself, "Bad luck will strike if the gift is not received in the proper way." She dried her tears, stood behind the window and let a high-pitched ululation burst forth, dancing to melodies of effusive joy. She hurried back to the room where the body was laid out and resumed wailing from the bottom of her heart. The affair reached the ears of some sly women and they whispered to one another and joked about it all Galila's life. It was passed around as a living testimony to the eccentricities of the controversial woman, who combined piety, love, and madness.

The death of her husband affected her sturdy constitution like nothing else. She mourned him with every ounce of her being and extolled his glorious deeds, real and imagined, for the rest of her long life. And she lived to 110! She lived through Muhammad Ali, Ibrahim, Abbas, Sa'id, Ismail, Tawfiq, the Urabi Revolution, and the 1919 Revolution. But no event lodged itself in her heart like the Urabi Revolution, which had counted her husband among its leading men. She would often relate his heroic exploits and imprisonment to her grandchildren, her imagination going to such lengths as to make Radia's sons and daughters believe it was Shaykh Mu'awiya who Arabized Muhammad Ali and upon whom Urabi had depended after God. The picture of Urabi in her mind became mixed with Antara, Hilal, and the family of the Prophet while honoring above all the memory of Shaykh Mu'awiya.

Of her children, only Radia and her sons and daughters brought her joy. She was pleased with Amr, although she only visited Bayt al-Qadi a few times, owing to old age. As for Shahira, Sadiqa, and Baligh, a wound that never healed settled in her heart. She would moan at Baligh as he lay drunk on the sofa in the hallway, "You're a drunk, a sinner, and disgrace to your noble clothes."

When his tree burst into leaf and he became an important merchant she said to him, "God has given you wealth to test you. Be careful."

Baligh loved her, but suspected she was not entirely sound in the head. Shahira had by this time returned to the family house as an outcast and filled it with cats, whereas Sadiqa . . . alas! What grief she suffered!

Qasim was Galila's favorite grandchild. He would cover her with kisses and listen to her stories, trusting in her with his heart and senses. When what befell him came to pass she was not worried but said to Radia, "Rejoice. God has given you a saint."

In the last five years of her life, toward the end of the first quarter of the twentieth century—at the beginning of the 1930s—she finally succumbed to old age. Her window to the world was obstructed by the loss of both her sight and hearing, yet she remained alert and would recognize her loved ones by touch. Shahira looked after her as much as she could until she tired of it; she had more compassion for her cats than for her mother. She would complain about her to Radia whenever she visited, so Radia took turns with her sister and reminded her of the Prophet's bequest to mothers. "It's easy to preach. You live venerated in your house and leave me on my own to carry out the bequest!" said Shahira.

On one of her visits, Radia found the hallway teeming with cats, mewing and running about wildly, warning that something was amiss. She discovered Galila lying lifeless on the sofa. Shahira was asleep upstairs.

Gamila Surur Aziz

Bayt al-Qadi Square and its trees weighed down with pasha's beard flowers had never seen anyone more beautiful, except perhaps Amr's daughter, Matariya. She borrowed her ivory complexion and wide green eyes from her mother, but had a prettier clove-shaped mouth and a better figure. In contrast to her mother, she surged with vitality and levity and derived the fieriness that tinged her cheeks with pink from her father. She was ahead of her time, not in terms of education, for like her sisters and female cousins her share only went as far as obliterating illiteracy, but in the impulsive, uninhibited behavior her premature maturity and dark yearnings unleashed in her. She would linger at the window watering the flowerpots, strut about the area between her house and her uncle's next door in the half veil, and meet hungry glances with rebellious coquetry. As a child, she wandered about the square with her older brother, Labib, and as the years passed Qasim joined them. She was a few years older than Qasim, but as she approached adolescence he was the only one around for her eager heart to toy with. Whenever they were alone together she would play with him to arouse him out of his innocence, and he would comply, confused, intoxicated, and delighted, as though seeing the beauty of dawn for the first time. His twitching fingertips touched jewels, ignorant of their value. He was not yet thirteen when he prematurely fell upon the honey. He opened up to her soft hand, dyed with henna like a rose, and inclined amiably to the effusions of her burning breast. The frivolity set her brother Amir against her. He berated her until she wept in frustration.

"Remember you're her younger brother," his mother said.

"But our reputation!"

"I know my daughter inside out. She's a paragon of good breeding," said Zaynab with the calm that never deserted her.

When Amir overstepped the mark his father, Surur Effendi, said, "Leave the matter to me."

Surur Effendi tended toward tolerance and at the time was wondering why his brother Amr's son had preferred Iffat, Abd al-Azim Pasha Dawud's daughter, over Gamila.

"God will disappoint him. Isn't our daughter prettier?" he said to his wife.

"Isn't he the son of the mad Radia?" Zaynab said scornfully.

"My brother claims he is a Sufi but his desire to be close to the rich transcends his desire to be close to God."

The truth was that Gamila frightened the conservative families in the neighborhood, and they shrank from her despite her beauty until destiny brought her a newly arrived officer at the Gamaliya police station called Ibrahim al-Aswani. He was tall, slim, and dark skinned. He saw her and found her very attractive and, finding she had a good reputation, proposed to her without hesitation. Qasim knew only that his seducer and teacher had changed overnight, like an apple gone rotten. The girl he knew vanished and was overtaken by a sobriety that did not dissolve for some time. She was wedded to her groom at his house in Darb al-Gamamiz in a celebration brought to life by al-Sarafiya and the singer Anur.

It was not long before the husband's work took the new family away from Cairo. Years went by, and they rose and went to bed without the birth of a child. Surur Effendi died before he was able to see any grandchildren through Gamila. Meanwhile, matters transpired for Ibrahim al-Aswani. He was a Wafd sympathizer. His sentiments became known through the lack of zeal he displayed in executing his duties during the dictatorship and, in the end, he was dismissed. He had inherited twenty feddans so traveled to his family in Aswan and publicly joined the Wafd party. He was elected to the House of Representatives and remained a permanent member of the Wafd. After fertility treatment, Gamila gave birth to five sons, of whom Surur and Muhammad survived. Marriage transformed her frivolity into impressive composure, extraordinary gravity, and generous motherhood. Her ever-increasing corpulence became proverbial. Ibrahim al-Aswani was prone to agitation and mood changes, but she was an ocean capable of receiving high waves and surging emotions and absorbing them with patience and perseverance, so as to restore him to perfect calm and self-control. Thus, it was right that she should be the one to advise Matariya's daughter, Amana, that, "A wife must be a tamer of wild beasts."

When the July Revolution came, Ibrahim al-Aswani was sure his political life was over. He retired to his land and devoted himself to farming. His sons, Surur and Muhammad, had joined the air force, but this branch of the family was destined for irrevocable extinction: Ibrahim al-Aswani was killed in a train crash in 1955 when he was fifty-five and Gamila only fifty;

Surur's plane was hit in the war of 1956 and he perished; and his brother, Muhammad, followed in the war of 1967. Gamila was delivered from her loneliness and sadness in 1970, dying of stomach cancer at the age of sixty-three. At the time of her death she resembled a branch without shoots on a family tree.

Ḥa'

Hazim Surur Aziz

FROM THE VERY BEGINNING he was antisocial and reclusive. He would stand in front of the house, away from his brothers and sisters and cousins, and watch people coming and going from the alleys off the square. He never once entered his uncle Amr's house. Amr would laugh and say to Surur, "Your son Hazim hates mankind." He was good looking like his mother, small like Bahiga, and nearsighted to the point of blindness in his left eye. He was never seen laughing or excited. His brilliance became clear in Qur'an school and he was near to repeating the success story of his older brother Labib. He kept to himself and had no goal in life other than to succeed; his relatives from Ata and Dawud's families did not even know he existed. His outstanding achievements meant his father did not spend a millieme on his education and he entered the faculty of engineering with a remission of fees fully deserved. It was clear to his brother Amir that he did not know the prime minister's name, read the papers, or connect emotionally with any wave in the sea of events stirring the nation. "Do you think the world is just about study?" Amir asked him. But no one could draw him into a discussion. When Amir was martyred in his jihad, Hazim was perplexed, silent, and dejected. But he did not utter a word or shed a tear and it was not long before he resumed life as usual.

He graduated as an engineer in 1938 but, because of his disability, did not head for the civil service. Instead, he found a better job at the building contractors of Dr. Muhammad Salama, who had been one of his teachers at school. The engineering professor was impressed by him and liked him. He regarded him as a model of intelligence and action, who steered clear of trouble. He would visit his teacher at his villa in Dokki and carry out various tasks, and there got to know Samiha, his daughter. Samiha was acceptable looking, but more importantly she was the daughter of his manager and teacher. He noticed the bey encouraged the acquaintance and this surprised him, given the man knew his humble origins and poverty. Nevertheless, he let vanity get the better of him until they were married and he had taken up residence in one of the apartments in a building the doctor owned and reckoned himself king of the world. The truth then began to emerge and he faced a situation that bespoke trouble: the bride's nervous side. She soon revealed a personality that was impossible to get along with. She was a hurricane that blew up and spread for the feeblest reasons, sometimes no reason whatsoever. He had a constitution that naturally deflected lightning bolts, inherited from his mother, Sitt Zaynab. He lived by his head, not his heart. Thus, seated in his living room, wrapped in navy blue silk robes and submerged in an armchair, he said to himself: So be it. The marriage is equitable at any rate. It promised him a future free of the need to dream while he possessed the intelligence and ambition to exploit what advantages there might be. If Samiha had been a perfect bride, or even just average, she would have married someone from the upper class to which she belonged, or a diplomat. Her father had given her to him after much thought and deliberation and he must accept the gift with similar thought and deliberation. He also said to himself: If she's the patient then I'm the doctor. And so he was.

The major deaths in Surur and Amr's families came in

succession shortly before the Second World War: first Amr, then Surur, then Zaynab. Samiha tired of visiting Hazim's mother, father, and siblings and decided in a moment of madness not to take part in the mourning ceremonies.

He looked at her pleadingly. "But. . . ."

His tone was loaded with meaning but she shot back vehemently, "I'm not going anywhere near that vermin-infested square. Nor do I want anyone from it coming to me."

He did not get angry and his face gave nothing away. Relations between him and his family were soon severed and he merged into her family, becoming a shadow of it and forgetting his roots. Yet his blind obedience did not guarantee him peace. Once, when he and his wife were alone after an evening in his apartment with his mother-in-law, her sister, and some of her relatives, she said to him, "I'm not impressed. You were too quiet. What few words escaped you were meaningless."

"Too much talking gives me a headache and no interesting subjects came up," he apologized with the utmost decorum and delicacy.

"So if we're not talking about engineering it's nonsense?" she bellowed.

He obliged her with a smile but she flew into a rage and roared the cruelest insults. She grabbed an expensive vase and hurled it at the wall. It shattered and the shards showered onto the embroidered sofa cover. He looked at her and smiled apprehensively then said affectionately, "Nothing in the world is worth you getting this angry about."

But the apartment also witnessed embraces and parenthood, and she gave birth to Husni and Adham. Hazim rose through the company, relying on perseverance and aptitude, and Muhammad Bey Salama relied on him increasingly as the days passed. Then, after the bey's death, he took his place as Samiha's proxy. He added to the capital with his own savings and, under him, the company prospered even more than it had previously. He built a villa in Dokki and his family moved there. He digested all Samiha's outbursts with extraordinary heroism, though some were difficult to stomach. For instance, Muhammad Bey Salama had been a member of the Wafd party whereas Hazim was indifferent to politics but, confronted with Samiha's zeal, would profess Wafdism in the home at least. His cool announcements were not, however, enough. He returned to the apartment one day to find a picture of al-Nahhas hanging in place of the picture of his father, Surur Effendi. He looked in silence without daring to comment. "I'm superstitious about pictures of the dead. This is a picture of the nation's leader," Samiha said. He said nothing, even when Muhammad Bey Salama and al-Nahhas died and their pictures remained in their places. On the day the family moved to the new villa she laughed loudly and said, "Praise be to God, you fool. We've raised you from the bottom to the top."

"Praise God for everything," he said submissively.

She frowned. "Don't forget the gratitude you owe me."

"You are generous and blessed," he replied with usual cool.

When the July Revolution came he worried his feigned Wafdism had spread beyond the walls of the house, but he was not exposed to any trouble. He assiduously applauded the revolution in the workplace while berating it at home in front of Samiha, his eyes scrutinizing his surroundings and seeking refuge in God. "Have you heard of a country ruled by a group of constables?" she would say in exasperation at every opportunity.

He would interrupt and whisper in her ear, "Be careful of the servants . . . the walls . . . the air. . . ."

How Samiha delighted at the Tripartite Aggression, and how her hopes were dashed. On June 5 she locked herself in her room and began to dance. When news arrived of the leader's death she trilled until Hazim stood up and, for the first time, shouted, "Have mercy on me!"

The company was nationalized but the rest of his family's

acquisitions were left untouched. During Sadat's era, Hazim reached his true zenith: he opened an engineering office and became a millionaire. Samiha said of the new leader, "His face may be black but his heart is white." Yet the defeat she suffered at the hands of her son Husni was probably more savage than her political defeat. From the outset she tried to control her children as she did their father but failed completely. Husni broke all barriers and shackles whereas Adham lived up to her dreams after he created a life for himself away from everyone. Samiha found no one on whom to vent her anger but Hazim. "If it weren't for your weakness and idiocy things would have been different," she said with contempt. In old age she fell victim to depression and was forced to convalesce for a month at a sanatorium in Helwan. Hazim remained healthy despite developing diabetes and was indeed rather pleased to be living with a sick wife; indeed he had long wished her dead, especially after the death of his patron. Strange dreams would entice him; he would see her the victim of a car accident or chronic illness, or drowning in the Mediterranean, or . . . or . . .

But he stopped having the dreams. The house was deserted when she was in the sanatorium, and he believed he had realized his eternal dream of success and fortune.

Hamid Amr Aziz

From the beginning he was an irregular plant in the family's soil. Amr Effendi probably did not slave as hard in raising any of his children as he did Hamid. He liked playing and fighting, acquired a wealth of vocabulary from the lexicon of street talk, and was routinely aggressive with his siblings, despite ranking sixth among them. As a result, he stumbled through Qur'an school and primary and secondary school and often returned to the old house with a torn gallabiya or a bloody nose, risking confrontation with his older brother, Amer, who had no qualms about beating him from time to time. Amr Effendi, on the other hand, made do with chastisements, gentle advice, and threats, while Radia endlessly resorted to spells and incantations and scattered vows about saints' tombs on his account. He harbored wicked intentions toward the girls in the family—like Gamila and Bahiga, his uncle's daughters, and Dananir, his aunt Rashwana's daughter—but his bad reputation put their mothers on guard. He also stood out in the family with his heavy build and large distinct features, which granted him manhood early. His greatest dream was to lead a gang like the celebrated strongmen who brought misery to the ancient quarter.

When, after several attempts, he attained the higher certificate, Mahmud Ata al-Murakibi advised his father to cut the path short and enroll him at the police academy: "It's the solution I've found for my son Hasan."

Amr Effendi welcomed the advice and Mahmud Ata promised to use his unassailable powers of intercession as an important noble to overcome any obstacles. Thus, Hamid entered the college the same year as his cousin Hasan. Mahmud made known his wish that Hamid marry his eldest daughter, Shakira, and Amr was delighted, for it would cement his relationship with the Murakibi family in the same way his son Amer had cemented his relationship with the Dawud family. The marriage paved the way for a grandeur his withered branch of the family had never dreamed of and enforced his position on the towering tree; he was honored and pleased. Hamid was happy too, even though his fiancée's appearance did not satisfy his hunger for beautiful things. Only Radia was annoyed.

"What a lamentable choice," she commented.

"Give praise to God, dear woman," said Amr.

"Praise God, the only one we praise for loathsome things!" she retorted angrily.

"Happy houses are founded on roots and morals," said the man hopefully.

"And money! How frustrating!" she said with contempt.

Surur Effendi informed his brother of his displeasure and began inwardly interpreting the matter as Amr's indomitable desire to cling to the coattails of rich relatives; Mahmud Ata had only chosen a groom like Hamid for his daughter because he was conscious deep down of her insipidity and that if he didn't find someone humble, who would be fettered by the favor, nobody would come forward except a freeloader eager to get hold of her money and take advantage of her and her loot. When Sitt Zaynab accused Radia of not wishing them well, Surur said to her, "It's not just Radia. On the outside the deal makes it look like Hamid is the beneficiary, but in fact the real beneficiaries are al-Murakibi and his daughter, who couldn't find a groom to oblige. My brother's a good man, but gullible."

One of Amr's daughters was not pleased. When Sadriya heard the news she commented, "My brother's marrying a man!"

When the 1919 Revolution came, Hamid was in his final year at the academy. He inclined to the revolution with all his heart and was accused of spurring on the strike, arraigned, and put back to the first year. Everyone was competing to make sacrifices so Amr Effendi was not especially upset, but praised God his son had not been expelled and thrown into the street. By the time he graduated as an officer, Mahmud Bey's standing had risen, having pledged allegiance to the Crown, and he was able to have Hamid admitted into the interior ministry's central offices with his son Hasan. Shakira was wedded to him soon after, without any real outlay on his part. He moved from the old house in Bayt al-Qadi to the mansion on Khayrat Square, where he and his wife would occupy a small wing on the private middle floor belonging to Mahmud's family.

It was without question a revolutionary migration: the boy from the alley and its stagnant corners found himself from one day to the next in a tall mansion surrounded by a lush garden and adorned with objets d'art, statues, and sumptuous furniture, where the sweet, melodious language of hanems rang out, the tables were embellished with the finest food, and the air was scented with piety and culture, without a trace of Radia's mysteries. Hamid also found himself in a cage guarded by a tyrant, Mahmud Ata al-Murakibi, and a hanem of immense sweetness and beauty, Nazli Hanem. As for his cousin and life partner, she was the image of her father in terms of sturdy build and a replica of her mother in terms of culture and piety. He could not change his nature, however, having dealt with gangsters since youth, and would behave like a police officer with them when they went too far. It was impossible for love to breed in his little world. All his life he knew only transient pleasure. From the first weeks of marriage he revealed his true colors in both word and deed. He did not, of course, forget the cage and its two guards; he was more in awe of Mahmud Bey than of his own father and stood before him as he would the august heads at the interior ministry. He curbed his unruliness as much as he could and tried to teach himself to be content with his situation, but habit compels and the tongue betrays. The bride was alarmed and whispered to her mother, "He is very vulgar—the way he eats, drinks, and talks." The hanem was mistress of the house in the true sense of the word. She asked for wisdom and patience and told her daughter, "None of this prevents him from being a man of virtue."

She was a good mediator between the two parties, and no one knew a thing about what went on in the new wing. But the hanem soon encountered a new problem: Radia and Shakira's mutual loathing. Radia could not conceal her feelings and Shakira did not disguise hers. Nazli Hanem and Radia were genuine friends, but deep down Nazli believed Radia was dangerous. "Be careful," she said to her daughter. "Your mother-in-law knows all about magic and its secrets and the saints. I believe the stories of her fraternizing with ifrit. Treat her with all due respect and courtesy."

She would entreat Radia too, saying, "Forgive my daughter. For the sake of our friendship, wipe her mistakes on my face instead."

Amidst this sea of turmoil Shakira gave birth to Wahida and Salih and gained some comfort in her stressful life, though it remained one devoid of love or peace. Similarly, her ability to cause upset was extremely limited. When the two brothers, Mahmud and Ahmad, fell out and the family unity was torn to shreds, Amr feared his son would be swept along by a current of hostility that had nothing to do with him. He tried to resolve the rift and maintain good relations with both his uncles. He advised Hamid to adopt his—Amr's—position and not sever relations with Ahmad Bey and he worked on Mahmud Bey until he consented to this. Hamid was pleased, for deep down he was fond of his uncle Ahmad and thought his demand justified.

In the period leading up to the Second World War and the years that followed, Ahmad, Amr, and Mahmud passed away. Hamid sensed he was free of guardians, and his relationship with his wife became worse than ever. This made Wahida and Salih miserable as they were torn between the two parents. Shakira was the greater influence in their upbringing so they grew up cultured, knew application and piety, and never freed their father of blame. They condemned his boorish behavior toward their mother and, though they tried to appear as neutral as possible in front of him, it showed. He could tell what was said in private from the looks in their eyes and felt alienated and angry. He continued to show his mother-in-law the respect and courtesy she deserved, but she was nevertheless compelled to tell him, "It pains me the way you treat Shakira." He resented Shakira and imagined she had devoured the best years of his life unfairly. One day, as they heaped abuses upon one another and traded the usual cruel insults, she suddenly screamed through her tears, "I hate you more than death." He risked the dream that had long been tempting him and divorced her, apologizing to her brother Hasan, his cousin, friend, and colleague, "Forgive me but I couldn't take any more. Everything happens according to God's will."

He only returned to the old house in Bayt al-Qadi for a month. Radia stated her view, "The marriage shouldn't have taken place but you don't have the right to divorce, in deference to Wahida and Salih." Back at the mansion they suspected Radia's magic to be in some way responsible for the divorce and indeed the marriage's failure from the first day. Hamid moved to an apartment in new building on al-Manyal Street shown to him by his cousin Halim, Abd al-Azim Pasha's son, who lived in one of the other apartments. In the 1950s, when he was nearly fifty, he fell in love with a widow called Esmat al-Awurfla, who was in her forties. He married her and brought her to his apartment to begin a new life. Relations with Wahida and Salih weakened, but were not severed. When the July Revolution came he was pensioned off with the other police officers it viewed as enemies of the people; it was known he had always been a Wafdist at heart, but the revolution considered Wafdists the state's enemies too. He shut himself off at home with Esmat for a while, but when he discovered Samira's son Hakim was at the heart of things and had influence, he entreated him and was appointed a manager of public relations with Amr Effendi, adding an extra fifty Egyptian pounds a month to his pension.

He was quite happy with his life. His new wife was experienced in the ways of the world. She met his violent moods and vulgarity with excellent cunning and paved the way for a stable existence with no visible cracks. He never stopped visiting the old house nor loving his mother and his brother Qasim; their eccentricity delighted him and he always had fun with them. He would let his mother kiss his brow affectionately and bowed his head for her to perform spells on and recite Surat al-Samad over and some of the daily prayers she knew by heart. He would

question his brother about his stars and future, tour his childhood haunts, and read the opening sura of the Qur'an at al-
Hussein, which represented the beginning and end of his religious
life. He also visited his sisters' houses and his brother Amer at the
Dawud family residence. During this period, his relations with
Abd al-Azim's son Halim grew stronger, for the two suffered an
identical fate at the hands of the revolution. So did his relations
with his cousin Labib. He smoked hashish with the former and
drank with the latter. Their hearts united in criticizing the revolution, contempt for its men, and remembering the good old
days. His happiness was only disturbed by a nagging awareness
that Wahida and Salih harbored for him only a fraction of the
love he had for them and that they much preferred their mother.
He was moved by the tragedies of the nation and his family. He
lived through the October 1973 attack and in the period that followed began to feel weak. He was initially diagnosed with ane-
mia, but his wife learned from laboratory results that he had
leukemia and death was waiting at the door. He did not know
what hit him. He was moved to the hospital not knowing what
was going on. His wife, Wahida, and Salih were present for his
final hours of agony. As the end approached, he asked to see
Radia, but circumstances prohibited it for she was over a hundred and did not know her son was sick, nor did she find out
before she died. He gave up the ghost after much suffering, seen
off by the tears of his wife, Wahida, and Salih. But death did not
lighten Shakira's deep hatred of him.

Habiba Amr Aziz

If Bayt al-Qadi Square, the alleys that emptied into it, and the
towering walnut trees left a trace in the hearts of Amr and
Surur's families; if the minarets, dervishes, strongmen, wedding
feasts, and funeral ceremonies; or the fairy tales, legends, and
ifrit left a trace, it was the life that flowed through the blood and

hid beneath the smiles, tears, and dreams in the heart of Amr Effendi's fifth child, Habiba, who could never bring herself to leave the quarter in spite of dazzling opportunities. No one loved their father and mother, brothers, sisters, cousins, even neighbors and cats, as much as she did. She wept over every death until she became known as "the mourner." She kept memories and promises and was permanently intoxicated by the past and its happy times. Her beauty nearly matched Samira's but for a film on her left eye. Her share of education went as far as erasing ignorance, which would soon return due to disuse. She knew nothing of her religion other than her mother's popular version but was convinced that fervent love for al-Hussein was the best route to the Hereafter. When she was sixteen, one of her brother Amer's friends, an Arabic language teacher called Shaykh Arif al-Minyawi, proposed and she was married to him in Darb al-Ahmar. After one happy year together she gave birth to Nadir but the next year the man fell into the clutches of cancer and died.

"Oh darling daughter, your luck is dreadful!" Radia cried in anguish.

Habiba lived with her mother-in-law on the proceeds of shops in al-Mugharbilin and dedicated her life to her son—a widow though not yet twenty. She loved Nadir as any mother loves her child, but she loved him too with a heart that seemed created to love. When Nadir came to the end of Qur'an school at the beginning of the 1930s, Mahmud Bey Ata wanted to marry her to a village mayor in Beni Suef. The family welcomed the idea, but she would have to surrender Nadir to her uncle. She categorically refused. She would not give up her son and did not want to leave the quarter.

"You're mad. You don't know what you're doing!" said her brother Hamid.

"On the contrary. I know exactly what I'm doing," she replied.

Amr tried and Radia tried, but she would not change her mind.

Nadir graduated from business school during the Second World War and was appointed to the tax office. But he was known for his ambition from the start. He began studying English at a private institute. His mother worried about how engrossed he was in work at the office and the institute. "Why do you put yourself to all this trouble?" she asked him. But he had charted his course and nothing could stand in his way. Habiba's arid life was capped by middle age, then she withered and looked ill. She watched her son's ascent with pleasure but, though he begrudged her none of his money, she refused to leave Darb al-Ahmar for a new villa of his. When he left and moved to his marital home she plunged into a fearful loneliness from whose grasp she did not escape until death.

"It's what we raise them to do. You should be glad and praise God," Radia told her.

"I've sacrificed so much for him!" she said broken-hearted.

"It's like that for every mother. Visit Sidi Yahya ibn Uqab," Radia replied.

She was the last of Amr's family to pass away. She wept for everyone with renowned passion until her tears dried up. However, when it was her turn there was no one left to weep.

Hasan Mahmud al-Murakibi

He grew up in comfort in the grand mansion on Khayrat Square and on the farm in Beni Suef. It was as though Nazli Hanem was brought into the Murakibi family to improve its pedigree, which showed in the male descendants, including Hasan, who was known for his height, good looks, and sturdy build. The customs of the day and Cairo's magnanimity at the time meant not a week went by without exchange visits between Khayrat Square and Bayt al-Qadi Square. Mahmud Bey wanted his first son to study agriculture, which would benefit him later on, but, like his cousin Hamid, his approach to study was lax so the man had them both enrolled at the police academy. The 1919 Revolution flooded Hasan with powerful emotions, but he did not expose himself to the kind of harm Hamid suffered and it did not take long for him to join the rest of his family in its stance with regard to the revolution's leader and allegiance to the Crown. This also better suited his job at the interior ministry as it meant he was not, like Hamid, divided between Wafdism in private and the government in public. Thanks to his father's influence he never knew the hardship of working in the provinces. He did not defer to his father's wish and marry early. Instead, he lived a licentious life, capitalizing on the fascination occasioned by his colorful uniform, the abundant money brought by his rank, and the gifts bestowed on him by his mother. However, he yielded in the end and married a girl called Zubayda from his mother's family. She was wedded to him in an apartment in Garden City, where he enjoyed a standard of living that even the interior minister himself envied.

During the period of political turmoil he became famous for his violence in dispersing demonstrations. He weathered successive attacks in the Wafdist newspapers, which damaged his public reputation to an extent, but raised his credibility at the mansion and with the English and granted him exceptional promotions.

"You entered the academy in the same year but he's made the rank of captain and you're still a second lieutenant," Amr Effendi remarked to his son Hamid.

"He's a traitor. The son of a pantofle-seller," Surur, who was with them at the lunch table, said viciously. But Hasan and Hamid were friends as well as relatives and they became even closer when the latter married Shakira. Hasan was nearly killed during Sidqi's time when bricks hit his head and neck. He spent an entire month in hospital. He was the most aggressive of his

siblings toward his uncle Ahmad's family when the disagreement divided the two brothers. Indeed, he came to blows with
Adnan and beat him up at the mansion—a sad day in the history of the family. Hasan produced three sons, Mahmud, Sharif,
and Omar; all of them fine specimens of good looks and intelligence. By the July Revolution he was a general and very rich,
owing to his and his wife's inheritances, but the revolution pensioned him off as part of a police purge. He exited on the same
list as Hamid, though their friendship had broken down after
Shakira's divorce.

"We should sell our land. Fortune has turned on landowners," he said to Zubayda.

The losses he suffered with the revolution did not compare
with those of others in his class, including his cousin Adnan, but
he still found himself in the opposite camp. He began acting like
a supporter of the new revolution. He started selling off his and
Zubayda's land in bursts and used the money to set up a business
on Sharif Street. He managed it himself and his wealth flour-
ished. His sons, Mahmud, Sharif, and Omar, were educated in
schools of the revolution. They were saturated with its philosophy and filled with the heroism of its leader. Hasan did not
mind; rather, his sons and two brothers, Abduh and Mahir, provided a protection against the hurricanes of the day. His brothers
were probably the reason his business escaped nationalization in
1961. When the disastrous event of June 5 took place, Mahmud,
Sharif, and Omar had graduated as doctors and worked in government hospitals. The Setback that shook Nasser's generation
and dispersed it with the winds of loss and despair overtook
them. Thus, the leader had barely died and Sadat taken over
before Mahmud and Sharif emigrated to the United States to
launch successful careers in medicine while Omar secured a con-
tract to work in Saudi Arabia. Hasan found purpose and consolation for past defeats in Sadat and his infitah policy. He buckled
down to work and illusory wealth. He built a mansion in

Mohandiseen for himself and his wife and lived the life of a king, dreaming his sons would one day return and inherit the millions he had accumulated for them. His life ended in an accident in the 1980s: he was driving his Mercedes along Pyramids Road when it flipped and caught fire. They extracted his body from it, blackened, stripped of the world and its millions.

Husni Hazim Surur

He was Hazim and Samiha's first child. He had a sporty build, a handsome face, and a brilliant mind. He grew up in comfort in the villa in Dokki and graduated as an engineer in 1976. Like his brother, he encountered no problems in life and did not know the worry of party affiliations, and, like his father, he proceeded down the path of fortune and success in his father's office. Samiha tried to control him, as she did his father, but found him insubordinate. Like her, he would get worked up over the smallest things. She perceived a dangerous unruliness in him so was keen to arrange his marriage, but he told her clearly, "It's nothing to do with you."

"But you're just a child," she said angrily.

He laughed loudly and looked toward his father, who avoided his eyes.

"It's my life," he said.

"You don't know anything about a good marriage."

"What's a 'good marriage'?" he inquired sardonically.

"Roots and money. They're synonymous!" she shouted back.

"Thanks, then I don't need a fiancée!" he continued in his sardonic tone.

He fell in love with a dancer called Agiba from one of the Pyramid nightclubs and, as his feelings were more than a passing whim, suggested they get married.

"If it wasn't love I'd never accept the shackles of marriage," she said.

He was overjoyed, but she made it a condition that he allow her to continue her art, which he contemplated worriedly before saying, "Let's remain as we are in that case."

"No. Then we can both go our own ways," she snapped back.

He acquiesced in spite of himself and married her. His brother, Adham, was the first to know, his father the second. When the news reached Samiha she raised a storm that brought the servants running and prompted inquiries from the neighbors. Husni moved to an apartment his wife owned on Pyramids Road.

"I haven't given up my art because the cinema has started to take notice of me," she said to him.

However, it became clear that the path to recognition was not easy and required him to set up a production company for his wife's genius. He knew his father no longer had the confidence in him that he used to, so asked for his share of the business capital to dedicate to the new venture. His father granted the wish, saying, "Keep it between you and me." With this, Husni cut himself off from his mother, and indeed the whole family. He produced two films for Agiba, neither of which brought her fame. Reports of a suspicious relationship between her and a supporting actor called Rashad al-Gamil reached his ears. He watched the two until he caught them in a furnished apartment in Agouza. He beat her to death and was charged and sentenced to fifteen years. Relatives learned his news from the newspapers and, before that, from gossip. More than one of them exclaimed, "Lord have pity! Son of Hazim, the son of Surur Effendi, God have mercy on him."

Hakim Hussein Qabil

Anyone who looked into his wide brown eyes was dazzled by their beautiful shape and bright shine, and his large head and thick hair lent him dignity. He was the third child of Amr Effendi's daughter Samira and her husband, Hussein Qabil, the antique dealer in Khan al-Khalili. Ibn Khaldun Street, where his family lived in an apartment block, was the amphitheater of his childhood and youth, al-Zahir Baybars Garden his playground. As well as being intelligent and a high achiever, he was fond of gambling from an early age, starting with dominoes and backgammon and later gravitating to poker and rummy. He was known for his close friendship with one of the neighbors. They were together through primary and secondary school, then Hakim went to the faculty of commerce, the other to the war college. Hakim knew all his mother's relatives—the families of Amr, Surur, al-Murakibi, and Dawud—just as he did his father's. His uncles Amer and Hamid were baffled by his political stance, which rejected, or seemed to reject, the situation in its entirety.

"I think the treaty is a great achievement for the Wafd!" Hamid said to him.

"It has several negatives. I don't believe in political parties," he replied.

"The Muslim Brothers buy and sell religion and Misr al-Fatah are Fascist agents!"

"Not all of them."

"So what do you believe in?"

"Nothing."

Amer gave a light-hearted laugh. "A dissonant chord in the family," said Hamid.

Hakim graduated during the Second World War, not long after his father died, and was appointed to the tax office. It was not long before he fell in love with a colleague called Saniya Karam, married her, and moved with her to an apartment in West Abbasiya. She gave birth to Hussein and Amr and life looked set to follow the familiar routine from start to finish. Then came the July Revolution and his best friend was one of its star players. The future hatched new dimensions no one would have imagined. At an opportune moment he was appointed manager of the distributions office at one of the major newspapers and his salary leaped from the tens to the hundreds with a stroke of the pen. His position sent ripples through the family tree from bottom to top. Samira's family cried for joy and Amr's family were pleased in spite of their shattered Wafdist dreams. As for the antagonists in the Murakibi and Dawud families, they remarked sarcastically, "Corruption used to be humble. Now it's greedy."

Because of his connection to his close friend he was revered, even by ministers, and flattered by friends and enemies alike. Within a short time, he moved to a new apartment in East Abbasiya, purchased a car, and became a true man of the times. He was loyal to family and friends and extended a helping hand to his uncle Hamid and cousin Nadir. It was thanks to him that his younger brother, Salim, was dealt with humanely when he was interrogated prior to his incarceration. Likewise, he was the intermediary in the appointment of many of his friends as guards after members of the family were placed under supervision. He remained close to his friend even after the man ranked with the new leaders. Not a week went by without a domestic visit to his mansion, where they would discuss romance and memories in confidence. On one such occasion he asked his friend casually, "Isn't it about time you nominated me as a minister?"

"What's the value in being a minister? Your income would be cut in half," the man said.

"But. . . ."

The other laughed. "I'm telling you I already tried . . . ," he said and gazed at Hakim with a meaningful smile.

"I promise I'll give up gambling," he said.

"It's your brother Salim too," said the friend dejectedly.

Hakim gave up the idea of becoming a minister, but his star

continued to soar and he was elected a member of the national assembly. His light went on shining until June 5, when his friend was among those swallowed by darkness. Hakim's influence thus disappeared in one blow, though he managed to keep his job. The fall was a personal as well as public defeat; he tasted the bitterness of ignominy after the sweetness of glory and found the many snubs he suffered—including from those he had loyally rescued from insignificance—unbearable. His only comforts in the world were his two sons, Hussein and Amr, who had become officers in the cavalry. Around this time, he began to show symptoms of high blood pressure and to suffer the effects. Then came the calamity he had often had nightmares about: Amr was martyred in the War of Attrition. Unlike Saniya, Hakim tried to maintain his self-control and appear brave and accepting of fate, leaving his sorrow to congeal deep inside him like sediment in a vessel. He carried on as one leader died and the next took over. He lived through October 6 and was shaken by a delirium he had not felt since the happy days before June 5. But the blaze was soon extinguished when he received news that his remaining son, Hussein, had been martyred on the battlefield. The tension mounted and exploded without self-control, a show of bravery, or acceptance of fate, and killed him. These events took place as Radia hovered at the summit of her old age. The angels chuckled in the old house.

Halim Abd al-Azim Dawud

He was born and grew up in an elegant villa in East Abbasiya, the third son of Abd al-Azim Pasha Dawud. He had a pleasant face and sporty build and from an early age was devoted to fun and amusement, jokes, and riotous behavior. He was never known to utter a single serious word. His two older brothers were excessively serious and industrious, hence he would say, "I was created to restore balance to the family."

Abd al-Azim Pasha watched bitterly as he stumbled through school and told him, "You'll bring shame on yourself and the family." But Halim took no notice of censure. Of the family's characteristics he retained only pride, conceit, and arrogance— he even held his own family, along with Amr and Surur, in contempt and resented the successful among them. Only Amer, who was married to his sister Iffat, was spared his tongue. The Murakibi family he placed, despite their wealth, on the same level assigned them by the Dawud family because of their lack of education and their descent from a man who sold pantofles. Had it not been for the weight of tradition and the vigilance of his aunts, he would not have hesitated to seduce the pretty female cousins of his age, like Surur Effendi's daughters, Gamila and Bahiga, or Rashwana's daughter, Dananir. Hamid was probably the only person he was cautious around, on account of his strength and predisposition to violence. He resented him nevertheless, and they remained adversaries until the final stages of their lives, when all they had in common was misfortune. In childhood and adolescence, amid his mother's pampering, he gained mastery in swimming, football, gambling, wine, romance, and amusement. He was also distinguished by a sweet voice and would say with characteristic conceit, "Were it not for family tradition, I'd be a popular singer." After a long struggle with school, he decided to enroll in the police academy. The family, men and women alike, was not impressed. "We're a family of lawyers and doctors," his father said.

"I have no patience with studying," he confessed.

When he enrolled at the academy he found Hasan Mahmud Ata al-Murakibi in his final year and Hamid halfway through. In keeping with academy conventions, he had to execute duties for them humbly and obediently. It would have been easier for him to do this for a soldier. Once, the three were having a meal with Radia, removed from duties and obligations. They got into a discussion of origins, boasting jokingly to one another. He reminded them of their roots and they reviled him for his. "You may be pashas but you come from the soil," Hamid said to him. Radia was following the conversation, smiling. "At the end of the day we're all Adam and Eve's children, and there's no champion in the family to match my father, Shaykh Mu'awiya."

Halim regarded Radia as one of life's curiosities with her dervish ways, magic, daily prayers, and ifrit. "In a different life she would take her natural place among the madmen at Bab al-Akhdar," he said to his mother.

"Be careful not to insult the dearest person to me," Farida Hanem exclaimed.

Farida Hanem believed in Radia and whenever they met would ask her to read her coffee cup. When in her old age she guessed her end was near, she stipulated that Radia, and no one else from either her or her husband's family, should wash her.

Halim graduated an officer a year after Hamid and, thanks to his father, was appointed to special posts at the interior ministry and spent most of his service guarding amirs and ministers. The 1919 Revolution played out before him like an emotive film in the cinema; never in his life had he associated with anything but amusement, riotous behavior, jokes, and entertainment. His father and brothers were dervishes of constitutional liberalism, but he was a dervish of bars, nightclubs, and casinos. He never contemplated forming a family or sustaining any ties. He chose an apartment for himself in a building on Nile Street—the one he showed Hamid after his divorce—and decorated it with gifts from amirs and ministers. It bore witness to all manner of prostitutes and artistes. He did not hesitate, even when he rose in rank, to spend the evening on the houseboat *Monologist*, drinking, behaving riotously, and singing, then staggering home at dawn. Relations became strained between him and his father and two brothers, and some futile attempts were made to arrange a marriage. But as the days passed he conquered them with his jovial spirit; he assailed their hearts until they surrendered to him like an unavoidable evil, probably the most gratifying evil in the family.

When the July Revolution came he was transferred to the district inspectorate. True, he was luckier than Hamid and Hasan, but in old age he had to work hard for the first time in his life. Moreover, he let his contempt for the revolution be known from the first day. He wondered how people distinguished by nothing but their possession of weapons could usurp government. Did it mean then that brigands could become kings? What had happened to noble families? How could the rank of pasha be eliminated with a stroke of the pen? How should he address his father and older brother from now on? How could he give the military salute to officers of similar or lower rank? Worst of all, he found in the Murakibi family two officers in the second tier of rulers, and Samira's son Hakim was part of the ruling body! The world had truly turned upside down—the bottom now at the top, the top now at the bottom. Fires of jealousy and rancor raged in his heart. He glowered angrily at the new world glowering at him.

How great was his delight at the Tripartite Aggression! He believed the curtain would come down on the comedy and the situation would be put right. But the events that followed frustrated his hopes, and the leader turned to meet a new world of chivalry and valor. His father died in the 1960s, followed two years later by his older brother, compounding his exile and sorrow. His amusements and riotous behavior escalated unchecked. One night he was at a luxury apartment for illicit gambling and there was a police raid. He made his identity known to the head of the force, but was ignored and herded with the others to the police station in Qasr al-Nil. The matter did not end well: the interior minister summoned him and demanded he submit his resignation to avert something worse. So he resigned in spite of himself and found himself on a pension. In dark despair, he decided to curb his routine. Hamid suggested that Hakim could intercede to find him a job, as he had done for him, but Halim thanked him and declined. He would rather make do on his pension than debase himself before Hakim. He found a way of living on his pension and replaced whisky with hashish, as it was cheaper and had an adequate effect. With instinctive contemptuousness, he gave himself wholly to detesting and deriding the era and its men. After June 5 he decided to make the pilgrimage to God's Holy Shrine. Like most of his family, he was not religious, except in name, but he performed the pilgrimage nevertheless, then resumed his life completely unchanged. He calmed down a little but developed diabetes and did not possess the will to confront the demands it made on his diet. It got out of control and he suffered successive complications. One evening he telephoned his neighbor and cousin and said, "Come over and bring Esmat Hanem. I'm dying. . . ."

He passed away that night with Hamid and his wife at his side.

Khalil Sabri al-Muqallad

THE FIRST CHILD of Surur Effendi's youngest daughter, Zayna, Khalil was born and grew up in the family home in Bayn al-Ganayin. The standard of living was good, thanks to his father's relative rise in salary, and considered an improvement on his grandfather's, who died before Khalil's mother, Zayna, married. Of the grandsons, he was the one who bore the closest resemblance to his uncle Labib. He inherited his good looks from his grandmother Sitt Zaynab, as well as his mother, Zayna, who was pretty—albeit less so than her sisters, Gamila and Bahiga. Zayna would sadly compare his face with his younger sister Amira's, for the girl had inherited from her mother a nose that spoiled her sweet face; the skies of her female future were clouded with fear, but it would not be long before death snatched her away after an acute stomach infection. Khalil displayed aptitude in school and was infused with the zeal of Nasser's generation. He had an unusual romantic experience in the final stage of secondary school when a relationship developed between him and a neighbor, a widow in her thirties called Khayriya al-Mahdi, who was fifteen years his senior. One evening, Zayna said to her husband, Sabri al-Muqallad, "Khayriya al-Mahdi has seduced your esteemed son!"

Sabri was at first startled. He was a broad-minded man and a devoted and understanding father. He had himself run wild in youth before marriage miraculously tamed him. The news alarmed him but it also aroused his pride. He watched the boy to make sure he was visiting the widow's house.

"You're not doing anything," Zayna said to him.

"Do you think advice would do any good?" he asked her.

"She's my age," she said anxiously.

"He'll soon be satiated and move on."

"I can't stay silent," she confessed. "Do you think they're thinking of getting married?"

The man couldn't help laughing. "The imbecile!" he exclaimed.

He began making inquiries to ascertain some facts. "The woman is rich," he told Zayna.

She sensed he was beginning to welcome the idea so appealed for help to her brother Labib. His public and private life did not leave him room to take on new problems, but at the same time he could not ignore his helpless younger sister. He graciously visited Bayn al-Ganayin, gathered the son and his parents together, and set the matter out plainly. The discussion did not yield a result that pleased Zayna.

"It won't affect me continuing my studies," said Khalil.

"Praise God. The bride may be old but she has plenty of money," said Labib, addressing Zayna and bringing the subject to a close.

Zayna wanted the marriage postponed until Khalil finished law school, but the bride was too keen to wait and it was only delayed for as long as it took for the woman to renovate and furnish her house. She married Khalil, and by the time he attained his law degree in 1965 he had a son, Uthman. He was appointed to the legal department. Many predicted the marriage would end in failure in due course, but Khayriya died undergoing surgery in al-Kulwa when she was fifty. She bore no other children after Uthman. Khalil never thought of marrying again.

Dal

Dawud Yazid al-Misri

HE WAS THE YOUNGER SON OF YAZID AL-MISRI and Farga al-Sayyad, born a year after his brother, Aziz, in the house in al-Ghuriya near Bab al-Mutawalli. Farga al-Sayyad was waiting for the right time to send the two boys to her mother at the market so they could learn to be fishmongers, but Yazid said, "I want them to attend Qur'an school first."

"Why waste time fruitlessly?" she protested.

"If I hadn't learned to read and write and mastered basic arithmetic I wouldn't have got my job at the paper supplier," said the man confidently.

The woman saw in selling fish advantages her husband could not get at the paper supplier, but she could not change his mind. Yazid found encouragement in his friend Shaykh al-Qalyubi, a teacher at al-Azhar. Indeed, he said, "Qur'an school then al-Azhar, Almighty God willing."

But Yazid's religion—like that of his other friend, Ata al-Murakibi, who lived in the same building—was satisfied by carrying out religious obligations, like prayer and fasting, and did not extend to deeper religious aspirations. Hence he conceived of Qur'an school for his two sons as a preface to working life.

One day, as the two brothers were wandering about between al-Ghuriya and the railway line they saw a band of policemen.

Aziz instinctively ran and hid, but the men seized Dawud and drove him away into the unknown. People discussed what they saw and knew the leader, Muhammad Ali, was taking people's sons off to secret locations to teach them new subjects and keeping them under guard so they could not escape education.

"If I hadn't been careful they would have got me too," Aziz said to his father.

Yazid complained of his "misfortune" to Shaykh al-Qalyubi.

"Don't be sad," the shaykh counseled. "Your son is safe and sound. Maybe it will protect him from harm."

The family was terribly upset. Farga cursed the leader. They began to watch more closely over Aziz, who continued to attend Qur'an school. Years passed. Aziz found work as the watchman of Bayn al-Qasrayn's public fountain and married Ata al-Murakibi's daughter, Ni'ma. Then, one day, Dawud returned to al-Ghuriya, his schooling complete. The family was overjoyed with his homecoming, but it was short-lived for he said, "They're sending us on a delegation to France."

"A land of infidels!" cried Yazid.

"To study medicine."

"If God hadn't been looking out for me I'd be going too!" exclaimed Aziz.

Dawud left to begin an experience he would never have dreamed of. During his absence, Yazid al-Misri and Farga al-Sayyad died, Aziz fathered Rashwana, Amr, and Surur, and Ata al-Murakibi leaped from the depths of poverty to the summits of wealth and moved from al-Ghuriya to the mansion on Khayrat Square. Dawud returned a doctor and headed to his old house in al-Ghuriya, where Aziz and his family lived alone. Affection united the two brothers once more. Aziz began observing his brother with interest and apprehension. He was happy to find him observing his prayers and still as fond as before of visiting al-Hussein, though his clothes had changed and, to a degree, so had the way he spoke. He seemed to be

hiding another side of himself that he had obtained in the infidel land. "Didn't they try to turn you away from your religion?"
Aziz asked him.

"Not at all," he answered laughing.

Aziz would have liked to talk to him more about "them" but
didn't want to upset the peace. He also asked, "Is it true you cut
bodies open?"

"When necessary. For the good of the patient," Dawud
replied.

Aziz praised God in secret for conferring flight on him that
day long ago.

"If things had been different you could be a father by now,"
he said to his brother.

"That's uppermost in my mind," Dawud said.

There was a Turkish family in Darb Qirmiz, the Rafat family.
He pointed them out and said, "Maybe they'd approve a doctor
returned from France for their daughter."

They decided that Ata al-Murakibi, in his new circumstances, was the right person to raise the matter. But Dawud was
refused as a vulgar peasant. Neither his knowledge nor his suit
or job could intercede on his behalf. The young man was hurt
and looked to his brother, Aziz, for guidance. "There's the War-
raq family that owns the paper supplier where our father
works," said Aziz. They were a family with Syrio-Egyptian
roots. The brothers found what they were looking for in the
great al-Warraq's granddaughter, Saniya. The family welcomed
the groom. The wedding was held and Dawud took his bride to
a new house in al-Sayyida. She gave him a son, Abd al-Azim,
and three daughters whom death snatched away as infants.
Dawud advanced in his profession until he earned the rank of
pasha and his official and intellectual standing was firmly established. It was destined that he should successfully reconcile his
two incongruous identities. In his medical profession he was
a fine emissary for the new civilization, with a vision of the

nation's future driven by a painful awareness of what the country lacked in his field and with close friends among both his Egyptian and foreign colleagues. Yet he was also in tune with his wife who, despite her beauty, social rank, and basic education, was not really any different from his mother, Farga al-Sayyad, and older brother's wife, Ni'ma al-Murakibi. He never renounced the customs of his family and environment, and visited the house in al-Ghuriya out of love and duty. There he would completely forget his assumed identity, sit at the low round table, tuck into the fish, bean cakes, lentil broth, salted fish, and green onions, and observe the love and affection developing between Abd al-Azim and Rashwana, Amr, and Surur. He visited al-Hussein and wandered around Bab al-Akhdar and got to know his brother's brother-in-law, Ata al-Murakibi, and two sons, Mahmud and Ahmad, and friend Shaykh al-Qalyubi, the father-in-law of Dawud's nephew Amr. During these times, he would revert to being the old Dawud, son of Yazid al-Misri and Farga al-Sayyad, son of al-Ghuriya and its fragrant, penetrating smells, towering minarets, and mashrabiyas clothed in the past.

Dawud wanted to make a doctor of his son, Abd al-Azim, to follow in his footsteps. However, the youth headed for law school, a school of ministers and the elite, and pursued an eminent and successful career as a lawyer. When the doctor pasha was fifty, he fell in love with a Sudanese maid and married her, prompting astonishment in the family and sparking gossip. He selected a separate house for her in al-Sayyida and set aside a grave in the family enclosure that Yazid al-Misri had erected near the tomb of Sidi Nagm al-Din, having seen it in a dream. His life extended until the Occupation. He and his brother were alive for the Urabi Revolution and supported it with their hearts, then swallowed its bitter failure. The brothers died in consecutive years early in the Occupation and were buried side by side in the grave inaugurated by Yazid al-Misri. It was not long before its female wing was occupied by Farga al-Sayyad,

Ni'ma Ata al-Murakibi, Saniya al-Warraq, and the poor maid in her special grave.

Dalal Hamada al-Qinawi

She was born and grew up in her parents' house in Khan Ga'far, the youngest child of Sadriya and Hamada al-Qinawi. Her house was a short distance from her grandfather Amr's, and she was as close to Amr and Radia as she was to her own parents. Like all the grandchildren, she adored Radia and was enchanted by her eccentricities, especially because her grandmother continued to pass on her innate heritage, clothed in supernatural phenomena, to each generation. "Dalal is beautiful but how did this Upper Egyptian accent infiltrate your Cairene children?" Radia would ask her daughter.

"From a mule!" Sadriya would respond scornfully, gesturing to her husband, whom she spent her life domesticating.

Radia would laugh, "He's as brainless as a stone, but he's respectable."

As was the custom, Dalal, like Nihad and Warda, was only permitted two years of Qur'an school before Sadriya assumed control of her education and instruction. Sadriya began to review the young men in the family—the sons of her sisters, brothers, and uncle, and descendants of al-Murakibi and Dawud. However, prospective grooms would also come to al-Qinawi's daughters from Qina and its environs in the name of the Qinawi family. A young village mayor called Zahran al-Murasini, who owned land adjacent to that of Dalal's father and uncles, requested to marry her. "It's destined that a train journey will come between me and my daughters," said Sadriya.

Dalal's sister Warda's tragedy delayed the marriage for a year. Then she was wedded to the village mayor in Cairo and, a week later, taken to his hometown. She settled in Karnak for good, gave birth to four daughters and three sons, and only visited Cairo on special occasions.

Dananir Sadiq Barakat

She was the only child of Rashwana, Amr and Surur's older sister, and Sadiq Barakat, the flour merchant in al-Khurnfush. She was born in Bayn al-Qasrayn in the house her father owned and grew up in considerable comfort, which looked set just to get better. Rashwana did not have any more children because of a defect in her, but, luckily for the family, Sadiq Barakat had two childless marriages behind him so he thought they were equally responsible. Dananir grew up between a mother who was as pious as a shaykh and a father whose family was regarded as pioneering in terms of female education. She was quite pretty and tended to be on the large side, which was considered an advantage. She also displayed promising energy in school. She obtained the primary school certificate and enrolled in secondary school, raising the eyebrows of Rashwana's uncle, Mahmud Bey Ata al-Murakibi.

"Do you approve of this?" he asked Amr.

"Her father does," Amr answered.

The man went to Bayn al-Qasrayn and assembled the family.

"I didn't let Shakira go beyond primary school," he said.

"Times have moved on, Mahmud Bey. The baccalaureate is appropriate nowadays," replied Sadiq Barakat.

"I have complete faith in my daughter's morals," said Rashwana.

Mahmud Bey had a sense of humor despite his boorish manner: "Raya and Sakina's mother probably once said the same about them." He left exasperated.

Dananir was delighted with her father's decision. The baccalaureate would put her on almost the same footing as Abd al-Azim Dawud's daughters, Fahima and Iffat. She would be way ahead of the daughters of her two uncles, Amr and Surur, and could hope for a suitable groom afterward. Rashwana took her to visit the family's roots and branches. She found the tree was heavy with fruit—Amer, Hamid, Labib, Hasan, Ghassan, and Halim. She was as pretty as any of the girls in the family, in her mind at least. But as she was coming to the end of school, something happened which she became convinced was the greatest tragedy that could befall a person: her father fell down paralyzed in the shop. He was carried home to lie helplessly in bed until the end. His business was liquidated under the supervision of Amr, Surur, and Mahmud Bey, and he received five hundred Egyptian pounds, all that was left, to pay for his medical treatment and sustain his family. Dananir realized there was nothing to look forward to but to finish her education and find a job. The Teacher Training College for Women was the only option and, at the time, female teachers could not marry if they wanted to continue working. This course of action was confirmed after Sadiq Barakat's death. Mahmud Bey saw things differently, however. "Let Dananir marry. I'll be your sponsor, Rashwana," he said. Rashwana was inclined to give her consent, but Dananir—driven by pride—refused and determined to choose her own destiny. Her decision did not make her happy; she had given up the dream of marriage she had entertained since she was a young girl. She was the most miserable person on earth, but at least she had chosen the misery herself.

"You have sacrificed yourself for my sake," Rashwana said.

"No, I've chosen what makes me happy," she replied firmly.

She became a teacher and spinster forever, finding comfort in her professional skills and immoderate eating. She went through life asking: Where did my bad luck come from? The eyes of many young male relatives and strangers gazed at her hungrily, as though wondering: Does this young woman who is forbidden marriage dream of romance? Her female cousins were all settled in their marital homes, even the ugly and masculine ones, whereas glances lingered on her and left festering scars. She went to bed each night after a hard day's work armed with a fantasy to relieve the loneliness. She persistently compensated her worries and sorrows with debauched feverish dreams, imaginary sins, and barren friendships with other dispossessed colleagues in her monastic profession. The secret life she lived in her fantasy world was utterly incongruous with her public life, which rested on earnest and praiseworthy work, a venerable commitment to religious obligations, and a sedate manner that disappointed any hopefuls but won their appreciation.

During this period of youth and activity, her uncle's son Labib—with his good looks, brilliant legal career, and for whom the road of conquest would have been easy were it not for his repugnant egotism—approached her. He invited her to the quiet Fish Garden and proposed an illicit relationship, which, in his mind, suited their circumstances.

"You're prevented from marriage and I'm avoiding it," he said.

She told herself angrily that he only wanted a girlfriend and did not see her as marriage material.

"A proposition for a prostitute!" she said with resentment and scorn.

He met the blow with the characteristic coolness he had inherited from his mother, Sitt Zaynab, while she returned to Bayn al-Qasrayn overflowing with anger at her whole family. They were wretches, rich and poor alike. They sold their souls without honor. This was how Amer married Abd al-Azim's daughter Iffat and Hamid married Shakira despite her ugliness. If the gaze of a young man from the Murakibi or Dawud family fell on one of Amr's or Surur's daughters all hell broke loose and their honor was roused. Wretches . . . wretches. . . . The Murakibi family sold their souls to the Crown to safeguard their interests and the Dawud family joined the Constitutional Liberals imagining they were following the path of noble families but their real roots issued from the soil; Dawud Pasha was merely the younger brother of Aziz, the fountain watchman! There was not a young man among them of her age, or older, who did not covet her honor, but none considered marrying her; a madman from al-Hussein was better than any of them.

Yet this period of verdant youth was not devoid of a respectable marriage opportunity in the form of her headmaster, who suggested she resign and marry him. But although she rather liked the idea, she quickly rejected it, maintaining that her mother would live at the mercy of someone from a wretched family who worshiped money and rank and would do anything to get it. Thus, she carried on her tedious, arid life, educating other people's daughters and preparing them for marriage, divided between illicit fantasies and a reality characterized by seriousness, piety, and respect. The tree of youth thirsted in the gloom of loneliness, the pain of deprivation, and the frivolous amusement of forbidden fantasies. Then its leaves began to fall one by one, leaving their mark in her excessive corpulence, coarsened features, flabby muscles, and overwhelming bitterness. During this time, Amr, Surur, Ahmad, and Mahmud passed away and many things changed beyond recognition. Her mother developed heart disease and took to her bed.

"I'll never forgive myself for what has happened to you," said Rashwana.

"I chose what suited me," she answered smiling and feigning cheerfulness.

"Marry at the first opportunity," Rashwana begged.

"It won't be long," she lied, for she no longer turned anyone's head.

Death came to Rashwana as her daughter was bringing her her evening apple. Dananir instantly grasped what was happening. "Don't leave me on my own," she cried. The woman breathed her last with her head propped against her chest. Dananir burst into tears and sent the old maid to fetch Radia from Bayt al-Qadi. With her mother gone, she suffered total solitude in Bayn al-Qasrayn. She became a picture of obesity and gloom. When the July Revolution arrived she saw it as just revenge for the tyrants, the weak, and the opportunistic. She lived it with listless satisfaction, for listlessness had subsumed everything, including her secret world and barren games. She plunged alone into the whirlwinds of the revolution with the radio, then television; it fanned the coals of her listless soul but it quickly passed. She was pensioned off and took shelter in the darkest loneliness with no comfort in the world except worship and Qur'an recitation. One leader died and another assumed power. New events swept in. The infitah policy came, and she suffered rising prices besides loneliness and old age. She began to prepare for her reckoning, asking herself: Could I be destined to suffer more troubles from this life? Can the future really conceal anything worse?

Radia Mu'awiya al-Qalyubi

THE FIRST CHILD OF SHAYKH MU'AWIYA al-Qalyubi and Galila al-Tarabishi, she was born and grew up in the old house in Suq al-Zalat, followed by Shahira, Sadiqa, and Baligh. Sadiqa was the most beautiful of the three sisters but Radia had the strongest personality and sharpest mind, as well as a good share of beauty. She was tall and slender and had a high forehead, straight nose, black almond eyes, and wheat-colored skin—the image of her mother. The shaykh was anxious his children should have a religious upbringing and she was the most receptive, for although in theory she only got as far as knowing the prayers, fasting, and memorizing a few of the Qur'an's shorter suras, her heart was permeated with love of God and the family of the Prophet. Yet she learned from her father only a fraction of what she learned from her mother in the way of mysteries, supernatural phenomena, the lives and miracles of saints, magic, ifrit, the spirits that inhabit cats, birds, and reptiles, dreams and their interpretations, astrology, popular remedies, and the blessings of monasteries and holy men and women. Her faith in her mother was only enforced by the confidence her father, the Azhar scholar, had in her medical prescriptions and incantations, and the fact that he kept the amulet she gave him around his neck.

Radia had a nervous temperament and alternated between love and antipathy dozens of times in a day. The hallway of the house—the site of the stove and well, the hub of daily life—witnessed the sway she held over her two sisters and her mother's bias toward her, which stirred the resentment of the other two. She had barely turned fourteen when Shaykh Mu'awiya's friend, Aziz Yazid al-Misri, asked for her hand for his son, Amr Effendi, who worked at the ministry of education. At the time the shaykh was isolated in his house, having completed the prison term he had been sentenced to for his part in the Urabi Revolution. The joyless life he had been living under the Occupation found its first occasion to celebrate. But fate did not grant him respite, for he passed away before he could prepare his daughter's trousseau; the bridal hamper was brought to his house the same day he died, prompting Galila to trill and wail in consecutive moments and making her a joke throughout the quarter. Radia's wedding thus lacked the usual rejoicing. She moved to the house on Bayt al-Qadi Square that Amr had prepared for their married life.

Amr was twenty years old, tall, of medium build, had a thick mustache and distinct features, and was perfectly disposed for married life. A strong conjugal love, capable of withstanding the ups and downs of life and contradictions of habit and temperament, quickly developed between the couple. At the same time, Radia made friends with Rashwana, her husband's sister, but not Ni'ma al-Murakibi, her mother-in-law, as though she guessed what had gone on behind her back when the two women came to propose. On the way back Ni'ma had said to her daughter, "The younger sisters are prettier!"

"The bride is very suitable. Thank God!" said Rashwana.

"I'm worried she'll be taller than Amr," Ni'ma said dubiously.

"No. Amr's definitely taller, Mama," Rashwana replied confidently.

In any event, Radia intuitively surmised that Ni'ma had held back with her and from the outset was quick to jump to the defense or launch an attack if the occasion arose. Yet God always granted salvation and nothing that warranted gossip passed between the two women. The men and women of the family came to meet and make friends with Radia: her brother-in-law, Surur; her father-in-law, Aziz; Doctor Dawud, his wife, Saniya Hanem al-Warraq, and son, Abd al-Azim; Mahmud Ata al-Murakibi and Nazli Hanem; and Ahmad Ata al-Murakibi and Fawziya Hanem. She had expected to be introduced to women like herself or whom she would outshine as she did her two sisters but instead was confronted with hanems from a higher class. The hanems' gentle natures and fine breeding and the fact that, despite appearances, they shared the same attitudes perhaps eased some of the disparity, but when she returned their visits with Amr she became increasingly conscious of the differences. She saw the doctor's house in al-Sayyida and cried in admiration at the legendary splendor of the mansion on Khayrat Square. There she realized her trousseau was utterly worthless. How she dreamed of a bed with four legs and a wooden headboard, a mirror in the reception room with a frame adorned with ornamental flowers, and a Turkish chaise longue. How she dreamed of furniture like those dazzling objets d'art. She felt defeated. "I'll tell you what I saw . . . ," she said to her mother in a tone of confession. Galila listened to her in silence, then asked with disdain whether there was among them a hero of the Urabi Revolution like Shaykh al-Mu'awiya?

Radia soon recovered her self-confidence and began telling the hanems about her heritage of mysteries and miracles. Thanks to the hanems' good manners, the new relationship was perfumed with rose water, and genuine affection sprang up on all sides. Radia's eccentricity was an added merit in this respect as it meant she always had an irresistible effect.

A power struggle emerged between husband and wife. Amr wanted his bride to remain in the house and not cross the threshold unless accompanied by him, whereas Radia felt her hidden knowledge required her to visit the tombs of the saints and the Prophet's family regularly and she warned Amr not to obstruct it. Amr was a member of the Sufi Dimirdashiya brotherhood and believed in her speculations and heritage. He feared the consequences of going too far, so he allowed her to move about freely, seeking goodness and blessing from it, confident of her morals, and satisfied with her exceptional skill in running the house and absolute dedication to his well-being. Things ran smoothly and no dispute between them ever lasted more than a few hours; when Amr was angry she was soothing, and when her nerves erupted Amr was forbearing and tolerant. Her standing among the upper branches of the family was well established even before it was reinforced with marriage ties. She assisted Saniya al-Warraq in arranging Abd al-Azim's engagement and Ni'ma al-Murakibi in arranging Surur Effendi's. As the days went by, she gave birth to Sadriya, Amer, Matariya, Samira, Habiba, Hamid, and, lastly, Qasim. She never stopped disseminating her superstitions among her children, as well as the branches of the family and neighbors, and became known as the quarter's Lady of Mysteries. She was known too for her pride in her father's heroism, owing to which she turned Urabi and his revolution into a legend of miracles and supernatural phenomena, intermeshed with miracles of the Bedouin, Abul Abbas, Abul Sa'd, and al-Sha'rani, and blended with Antara, Diyab, ifrit, magic, charms, amulets, incense, and spells. She had no qualms about speaking frankly to Dawud Pasha. "This medicine of yours is useless and no good," she would say, or, "There is one doctor with no equal and that's God the Almighty."

The pasha enjoyed her conversation and went along with her, although he would sometimes tease, "But Sitt Umm Amer, you appoint other saints and ifrit as gods alongside God."

"Never!" she would reply with conviction. "His will is behind all things. If it wasn't for Him my master al-Naqshabandi could not be in Mecca, Baghdad, and Cairo at the same time!"

She and Amr shared similar beliefs so they always enjoyed conversation and mutual understanding. She watched the 1919 Revolution through the mashrabiya of the old house and registered a new saint called Sa'd Zaghloul in her timeless dictionary. When Amr took part in the civil servants' strike she asked herself anxiously, "Will they imprison him like they imprisoned Shaykh Mu'awiya?" She cut through streets swelling with riots and visited the tomb of Sidi Yahya ibn Uqab and invoked eternal damnation upon the English and their queen—for she believed Queen Victoria was still alive. She was beset with anxiety over Amer's role in the demonstrations and Hamid's punishment when he was accused of spurring the strike at the police academy. "Lord save us from these evils! Lord let the oppressed triumph!" her tormented heart cried at the tomb of al-Hussein.

She educated her children in her heritage, then when everyone began talking about the nation and Sa'd and the field of consciousness expanded, events became their principal educator. She kept her health and, like her mother, lived beyond a hundred. Meanwhile, her children became families and grandchildren grew up. She heard of a new leader called Mustafa al-Nahhas and eventually Gamal Abdel Nasser, who was the last leader she would know and who raised her grandchildren to the skies then plunged the greatest among them into destitution or jail. Thus, she blessed and cursed him alternately. During her lifetime, her own mother and sisters, Ahmad Ata, Amr, Surur, and Mahmud Ata perished, as did others she did not know about. Two events affected her more than any other: the death of Amr, whom she grieved over for the rest of her life, and Qasim's tragedy, especially in the beginning. Yet she stood firm with unusual strength and overcame her worries with a rare energy. She did not retire to her house until she was over a hundred and, even then, continued to shuffle about in the hallway until her final year. When the end was decreed, death came kindly and gently. Sadriya sat cross-legged at the end of her bed. She heard her mother sing in a feeble voice, *"Come back to me, O night of greatness, come back."*

Sadriya laughed and asked, "Are you singing, Mother?"

"I'm singing this song and dancing between the well and the stove," Radia replied.

Her head inclined to the left, and she sought refuge in eternal silence.

Rashwana Aziz Yazid al-Misri

She was the first child of Aziz Effendi and Ni'ma Ata al-Murakibi. She was born and grew up in the family home in al-Ghuriya where Yazid al-Misri lived on the first floor and Ata al-Murakibi, her maternal grandfather, on the second. It was obvious when Amr and Surur were born that the two boys were better looking than their sister, but Rashwana was not ugly and she had a fine figure. Her father cast her loose with her brothers, but she trained hard at housework. By nature, and with her mother's influence, she inclined to piety and was known throughout her life as God-fearing and devout. When she was fifteen, Sadiq Barakat, a flour merchant in al-Khurnfush, wanted to marry her. He was a business associate of Ata al-Murakibi and through him had got to know Aziz, the fountain watchman and husband of Ata's daughter, Ni'ma. Sadiq asked for the hand of Aziz's eldest daughter and she was wedded to him at the house he owned in Bayn al-Qasrayn, a short way from her father's fountain. Sadiq Barakat had been married twice before but had no children, and years went by without Rashwana falling pregnant. Then she gave birth to their only daughter, Dananir, and everyone rejoiced, Sadiq Barakat most of all. His financial situation was good, much better than Ata al-Murakibi's or Aziz Yazid al-Misri's. Rashwana's life was pleasant, her kitchen filled to capacity, and her veil ornamented with gold. She would visit her parents in al-Ghuriya and brothers, Amr and Surur, in Bayt al-Qadi laden with gifts.

Dananir was similar in looks to her mother, perhaps a little prettier. She displayed talent at school so her father encouraged her to continue, despite Mahmud Ata al-Murakibi's objections. Rashwana supported her husband's plan so that her daughter could keep abreast of Fahima and Iffat, the two daughters of her cousin Abd al-Azim Dawud, although she envisaged marriage as the happy ending to education. Thus, she trained Dananir in housework during the long school holidays and waited anxiously for a suitable man. When Sadiq Barakat's tragic illness confined him to his bed, she accepted that there was no alternative except for Dananir to continue her education, at least until she was able to marry. The need for this intensified after Sadiq Barakat died and she lost her source of income. She would not have seen any harm in Dananir marrying with the proviso that her uncle, Mahmud Bey, support her, had her daughter not refused and insisted on work, even if it meant being deprived of her legitimate right to marry. Rashwana's father, Aziz, had died leaving her nothing to support herself with, and her mother, Ni'ma, died poor because Ata al-Murakibi's fortune came to him from the wife he married after Sakina, his first wife and Ni'ma's mother, had died. (Sakina was the daughter of the owner of the pantofle shop that Ata inherited—or rather managed on his wife's behalf—and liquidated when she died.) Rashwana hated the thought of Dananir sacrificing herself for her sake and tried in vain to bring her round to her uncle Mahmud's generous offer, which his brother, Ahmad, most gladly joined him in. But Dananir refused, saying, "We'll keep our honor even if it costs us."

She did not conceal her abiding criticism of her uncle and the rest of the family from her mother. "They worship money and rank and have no honor."

"You're a harsh judge! They are good, God-fearing people," Rashwana said in dismay.

"You are good. You judge them generously. There's your mistake," Dananir replied gently.

Rashwana conveyed her anxiety to everybody—her brother Amr, Radia, Nazli Hanem, Fawziya Hanem, and Farida Hanem Husam, Abd al-Azim's wife. Not one of them endorsed the girl's pride. They predicted she would end up regretting it when there was no need, while Radia asked herself: Who is the infidel who prohibits women teachers from marrying?

Rashwana eyed her daughter worriedly, trying to plumb her depths, inquisitive of her thoughts and emotions, of what was hidden in the folds of her peculiar life, which resembled a man's.

Whenever Dananir was stressed or complained about a work-related matter, Rashwana interpreted it in terms of some other cause lurking beneath of her irregular, meager life. She watched as her daughter grew fatter day by day, lost her graceful youth and looks, and assumed the marks of seriousness and coarseness. It was as though work had unwittingly transformed her into a man. Rashwana was alone with her brother Surur Effendi in his house on Bayt al-Qadi Square.

"God bless you, Brother. Why don't you take Dananir for your son Labib?" she asked.

"But she doesn't want to leave you at the mercy of others," Surur replied evasively.

"I could convince her if she had the good fortune of finding a groom like your son."

"The truth is I don't really want Labib to marry until Gamila, Bahiga, and Zayna have found husbands. I only have a small salary and his assistance in the girls' trousseaus is indispensable," he told her frankly.

She returned, with a lump in her throat, to ruminate on her worries, which only ever left her at prayer times. She watched and saw her daughter's youth vanish completely, its place taken by a gloomy picture marked by coarseness and barrenness; no one doubted that it was the specter of a spinster whose life was ruined. Her worries piled up as loved ones died one after the other: Ahmad, Amr, Mahmud, and Surur. Then her heart had to bear disease as well as constant sorrow. She took to her bed reluctantly and spent her nights in agony, aware death was on its way. . . . The Murakibi and Dawud families came by and Amr and Surur's families visited regularly. She bequeathed Dananir to every one of them. She said to her daughter as though imparting her final testimony, "Marry at the next opportunity."

In her dying hour Dananir rushed to her bed. She propped her mother's head against her chest and recited what verses she could remember from the Qur'an until the woman breathed her last, leaving Dananir alone in the true sense of the word.

Zaynab Abd al-Halim al-Naggar

SHE WAS BORN AND GREW UP IN AL-KURDI LANE in al-Hussein to an Egyptian father called Abd al-Halim al-Naggar, who owned a small carpenter's shop in the quarter, and a Syrian mother. She married Surur three years after his older brother, Amr, was married. Aziz believed in early marriages and had paid no attention to Surur's protests.

"Marriage is the best medicine for people like you," Aziz told his son.

"You're a lusty man but you're poor. Marriage is the cheapest way!" said his brother, Amr.

They sought the help of a matchmaker, who showed them to Abd al-Halim's house. The man had a good reputation and was financially well-off. Surur objected to the fact that he was a craftsman but the matchmaker said, "His daughter is well brought up and beautiful." Ni'ma and Radia made the customary visit and were truly dazzled by the bride's beauty. She was fair, with black hair, green eyes, a supple body, and a look of deep calm.

"A paragon of beauty," Ni'ma remarked on their return journey.

Radia's jealousy was ignited. "As far as roots are concerned, we're all children of Adam and Eve," she said in what seemed like support and resistance at the same time.

Zaynab was wedded to Surur in the house next door to Amr's on Bayt al-Qadi Square. The moment the veil was lifted from her face, he fell in love, and she loved him until the last years of her life and gave him Labib, Gamila, Bahiga, Zayna, Amir, and Hazim. Her beauty ensured a friendly reception in the family and its branches and the good impression was confirmed by her decorum, gentleness, and calm nature. She was instinctively conscious that Radia was jealous of her, but no complications proceeded from this thanks to her calm nature, which seemed to border on coolness. She always treated Radia with respect and friendliness. She put Radia before herself as the wife of her husband's older brother and always hoped Radia's sons would be her daughters' husbands. Whenever one of them headed in another direction she suspected Radia to be the reason he digressed from his rightful destination, from the girl with first claim to him. But this did not muddy the love between the two families and never came to the surface. Her real troubles began when Surur approached middle age. His restlessness and the way he gazed automatically at each and every pretty girl in the quarter did not escape her vigilant eyes, and so a dispute developed between them late in life. He deflected any accusations with anger and edginess, while she censured and complained in a low voice, with constant gentleness. When her patience ran out she complained to his older brother, Amr Effendi.

"People grow wiser with age," Amr said to his brother.

He assured him that his wife was always full of misgivings.

"Your children have grown up too," said Amr.

Radia learned of the problem and would say to her sister-in-law, "Where would he find beauty like yours?" But she was secretly pleased, telling herself that no woman can survive by beauty alone.

Zaynab was not spared the effects of sorrow, for she developed diabetes and high blood pressure. Illnesses visited her successively and pallor crept into her radiant beauty, snuffing it out bit by bit before her time. She constantly discerned hungry hopes in Surur's eyes and lived in an atmosphere heavily clouded with fear. She was alternately beset with the outright fear that, were he not poor, he would marry again, and the likelihood that he would find a rich woman who loved him as Ata al-Murakibi had been lucky enough to do long ago. How she envied Radia the contentment of her husband and her status among the family thanks to marriage ties with the Murakibis and Dawuds. "Look how they love your brother and shower gifts on him. You've driven them away with your vicious tongue!" she said to her husband.

The Second World War came with its darkness and air raids. However, the most abominable raid of all was the fate that swept down on Surur. His health deteriorated and he submitted to the hands of death prematurely, in his final year of service. The loss of the man she had never ceased loving for an hour of her life, despite the tepidity of his desire and sluggishness of his love, dealt Zaynab the final blow. One year after his death, she suffered a brain hemorrhage that rendered her unconscious for three days. On the fourth day, in Radia's arms, she passed away.

Zayna Surur Aziz

She was the youngest daughter of Surur Effendi and the fourth of his children. She was known for her wide green eyes and a body that was quick to ripen and looked more like an adult's than a young virgin's. She was confined to the house at an early age, after she had learned to read and write at Qur'an school, and progressed to adolescence waiting for a suitable man. Gamila departed for her marital home and Zayna was left behind waiting with Bahiga. Her youth unfolded onto her family as it was assailed by alienation and tension in an atmosphere of darkness and air raids. She noticed early on the romantic maneuvers between Bahiga and Qasim and knew with her sharp instincts that their similar ages made them unsuitable marriage candidates, that the young man should rather be looking at her. Sitt Zaynab tirelessly took Zayna and Bahiga on visits to the family houses. Countless eyes devoured her, yet it seemed no one considered either of them for marriage. The family easily deserved what the father repelled from it, and better. Illness overtook Qasim and he took shelter in his new world. Her sister Bahiga met the blow with silence, patience, and acceptance. Her father died, then her mother, and she was left alone with her sister, visited in passing by their brother Labib when his work outside Cairo allowed. "God does not forget any of his servants. Whoever trusts in God is not sorry," Radia told them.

One day, sitting with the two of them in his gallabiya, Labib said, "Someone has come and asked me for your hand, Zayna."

Her heart fluttered. She looked at her sister guiltily.

"Everyone gets their share at the appointed time," said Labib.

"You're absolutely right, Labib," said Bahiga. "Congratulations," she said to her sister, despite the despair engulfing her.

"For my part, I wouldn't miss an opportunity," said the man.

A heavy silence reigned. Then Labib, who was capable of confronting the most uncomfortable situations, said, "His name is Sabri al-Muqallad. He works in a chemical company."

"A company!" Zayna muttered dubiously.

"It's better than the civil service. The world is changing." Shaking his big head, he continued, "I've heard he is a heavy drinker and he admitted as much. But he has earnestly assured me that he has repented and is fit for marriage. What do you think?"

"It's your decision," she said submissively.

"There is no use for such talk today. You will see him for yourself."

Sabri al-Muqallad came and Labib received him in the old

reception room. Zayna made herself up and put on the finest clothes she owned and went in to meet her destiny. She could not examine his face closely but a glance was enough to glean a picture of him. He was very thin and had a gigantic nose, a big mouth, and a long face. When he left Labib said, "The man's ugliness doesn't mean he is no good. He has a good salary . . . a good family. . . . You have the final word." She knew she wanted a husband at any price; she could not stand her gloomy existence any longer. Let God take care of Bahiga. She was wedded to him in a house his mother owned in Bayn al-Ganayin.

She seemed happy with her marriage and gave birth to Khalil and Amira. Amira perished in infancy, leaving a deep wound in the heart of the youthful mother. Sabri was twenty years older than her but she enjoyed a pleasant life in his care, strutting about in the finest clothes and dining on the most appetizing food, until she became excessively fat and started to resemble Egypt's first chanteuses. Her son Khalil's marriage to a widow the same age as her shocked her, but she quickly got over her distress without any real crisis. The only blight on her happiness was the period she was separated from the rest of her family, when the traditional constant caravan of visitors was like a dream without a shadow of reality. Time brought the radio and television, Cairo swelled, and unexpected events, wars, and maladies poured down on the city. Bayn al-Ganayin, like other quarters, seemed to become an independent kingdom whose borders were only crossed in times of disaster.

Sin

Surur Aziz Yazid al-Misri

HE WAS BORN AND GREW UP IN THE HOUSE in al-Ghuriya in sight
of Bab al-Mutawalli with his older brother, Amr, and their older
sister, Rashwana. His childhood pastures extended between the
gate and Bayn al-Qasrayn's public fountain, where their father,
Aziz, perched on his aqueous throne. Surur resembled his
brother in height and distinct features, but his face disclosed a
finer symmetry and he tended to be fatter. His grandmother,
Ni'ma al-Murakibi, lavished him with a special affection, the
like of which was not enjoyed by Amr and Rashwana, and
spoiled him in spite of Aziz's objections and warnings. He grew
up a natural believer but, unlike the rest of his family, without
the trappings, and did not heed prayer times or fast until he was
fifty, a course his own family would later follow. He appeared to
be idle and hated studying so his progress was stilted. Meanwhile, the way he teased girls and his impulsiveness bespoke
trouble. He tried to drag his brother, Amr, along with him but
found him unresponsive; indeed, he found him obstructive and
reproachful. The two shared a strong fraternal love that ultimately withstood the disagreements which tarnished their relationship over time. He worked his way through primary school
with difficulty and Amr fared no better, so upon receiving the
primary school certificate he threw down his weapons and was

lucky enough to find a job in the railways. The primary school certificate was a significant document, so Aziz was satisfied and praised God. He had hoped for more for his sons, impressed by the example of his brother, Dawud Pasha, and nephew, Abd al-Azim, but told himself, "Contentment is a virtue." He began thinking about the next important step, namely marriage. When he discussed the matter with Surur he found him lukewarm. Aziz told him plainly he did not approve of his behavior and thought marriage the best remedy. Amr agreed enthusiastically with his father, and Surur soon yielded out of respect for them and because he was eager to experience the magic of marriage. The matchmaker showed them to Zaynab's house and a caravan made up of Ni'ma, Rashwana, and Radia set out to court her. She was wedded to him in the house next door to his brother's on Bayt al-Qadi Square.

Surur was dazzled by his wife's beauty, calm nature, and gentle disposition. With her he found love and gratification and, over the course of a prosperous marriage, she gave birth to Labib, Gamila, Bahiga, Zayna, Amir, and Hazim. Surur's government job, excellent wife, and beautiful children paved the way for equanimity. However, he always dwelled on what he lacked so was often corrupted by fantasies, and envy united his heart and tongue. He and Zaynab were united by something that she hid with her calm nature and gentle disposition and he revealed with his careless mannishness. He knew—it was impossible not to—what his grandfather Ata al-Murakibi had been and how he had become who he was, how destiny had smiled on him, just as he knew where his uncle Dawud's "Pasha" title came from. He objected to his grandfather's wealth and his mother's poverty, accusing him of depravity and cruelty, and he burned with jealousy of his beloved brother, Amr, because everyone showered affection and gifts on him while he, Surur, was ignored as though he were not Amr's brother, forgetting that it was his own vicious tongue that deterred people. His aggravation was compounded when Amr passed over his two daughters and married his two sons into the families of Dawud and al-Murakibi. Yet any resentment between the two brothers and their two families remained beneath the surface and love always conquered, even if deep down conflicting frustrations often surged. Even Radia and Zaynab's differences were concealed by ongoing peace and good relations. Surur wept passionately the day Amr died, and Zaynab passed away beneath an awning of Radia's recitation and tears.

In the same way that Surur was less pious than his brother, so he was less patriotic. However, the 1919 Revolution lodged in his insubordinate heart a warmth that would remain with him to his dying breath. He persistently boasted about his part in the civil servants' strike, as though he had been the only person to strike, and memories of the demonstrations lived on in his imagination as one of the delights he most savored from his life. The violent wave clamoring with anthems of glory swept with it father and son and burst into the hearts of the women behind the mashrabiya. He thus found in the Murakibi and Dawud families' renunciation of its hallowed leaders a target upon which he could unreservedly unleash his tongue. "We have an uncle who worships nothing in the world but his self-interest," he would say to his brother. Or, "The great house of Dawud has joined Adli under the illusion that they are really part of the aristocracy!"

In middle age another revolution exploded in Surur, which entailed a revolt against his wife's love. His eyes and impulses burst out in pursuit of adolescent fantasies and a rift developed between him and the meek, loving, sorrowful Zaynab.

"What will we do if one of our neighbors complains about you to her husband?" she would reprimand him in a whisper.

"There is nothing to complain about," he would retort.

When she complained to Amr, Surur poured anger on her and threatened he could marry again whenever he liked, though a second marriage was really an impossible dream. In fact he only betrayed his wife twice—once in a brothel, and then in a short fling that lasted no more than a week. He increasingly resented his poverty and his boorish grandfather even more. He tirelessly bought lottery tickets, but gained nothing from it other than the silent reproach glimmering in the eyes of his eldest son, Labib, and daughters, especially after Zaynab's health deteriorated. When Amr died, loneliness and depression descended on him, and when the war, the darkness, and the air raids came, he declared life a raw deal. His only consolation was his son Labib's success, but his constant boasting about it made him a heavier weight on the family's hearts. In later life, he stopped going to see the Murakibi and Dawud families but would often visit Amr's sons and daughters, just as he would his sister's house, and joined in their joys and sorrows. They had been fond of him since they were young, and became even more so when their own father died. One autumn evening in his final year of government service, as he sat behind the mashrabiya gazing out at the dark cowering above the houses and minarets, expecting the usual air raid siren to come at any minute, he had a heart attack. His life was over in less than a minute.

Salim Hussein Qabil

The last child of Samira Amr and Hussein Qabil, he was born and grew up on Ibn Khaldun Street. His father died when he was only a year old so he was brought up in a disciplined climate, nothing like the comfortable lifestyle his family had enjoyed when he was just a glimmer on the horizon. He was good looking like his mother and tall like his father, and had a large head and intellect like his brother Hakim. His obstinacy and stubbornness, as well as his talent in school, came to light in childhood. His sister Hanuma watched over him closely with her piety and strict morality, and for a long time he believed he was learning the truth about the Unknown from the lips of his grandmother Radia. He loved football and was good at it, enjoyed mixing with girls in al-Zahir Baybars Garden, and hated the English. Dreams of reform and the perfect city toyed constantly with his imagination. He did not incline to any one party, deterred by his brother Hakim, who rejected everything outright. He once heard Hakim say, "We need something new," and replied automatically, "Like Caliph Omar ibn al-Khattab."

His own temperament and Hanuma's influence prompted him to turn to the religious books in his brother's library. His dream of the perfect city vanquished football and girls. He was in secondary school for the July Revolution and welcomed it eagerly, like deliverance from annihilation. The role his brother Hakim played in it strengthened his commitment and, for the first time, it seemed to him the perfect city was being built, brick by brick. He thought that by joining the Muslim Brotherhood he could immerse himself further in the revolution, but when the revolution and the Brothers came into conflict his heart remained with the latter. Disagreement emerged between him and his brother. "Be careful," Hakim said.

"Caution can't save us from fate," Salim replied.

He entered law school and his political—or rather religious— activities increased. But none of his family imagined he would be among the accused in the great case against the Muslim Brothers. Hakim was dismayed. "It's out of our hands!" he said to his anxious mother. Salim was sentenced to ten years in jail. Samira reeled at the force of the blow; Hakim's shining star could not console her for his brother's incarceration. She secretly despised the revolution, and Radia invoked evil on it and its men.

Salim was released from prison a year before June 5, completed the remainder of his studies, earned a degree, and started work in the office of an important Muslim Brotherhood attorney. He saw the great defeat as divine punishment for an infidel government. He did not sever links with his accomplices but conducted his business with extreme secrecy and caution. He found relief in writing and devoted years of his life to it. His labors bore fruit in his book, *The Golden Age of Islam*, which he followed with a work on the steadfast and pious. At the same time, he achieved considerable success as a lawyer and, with the sales of his two books, his finances improved, especially after Saudi Arabia purchased a large number of them. When the revolution's leader died, he recovered a certain repose. Samira said to him, "It's time you thought of marrying." He responded eagerly, so she said, "You must see Hadiya, your aunt Matariya's granddaughter through Amana."

Hadiya was the youngest of Amana's children. She had recently returned from the Gulf after teaching there for two years and had purchased an apartment in Manshiyat al-Bakri. He went with Samira to Abd al-Rahman Amin and Amana's house on Azhar Street and saw Hadiya, a fine looking teacher in the prime of youth, whose beauty was very much like her grandmother Matariya's, the most beautiful woman in the family. Samira proposed to her on his behalf, she was wedded to him, and he moved to her apartment in Manshiyat al-Bakri. He had a lovely wife and flourishing career. He knew love and compassion under Sadat and had no cause for worry other than the new religious currents that had emerged within the Brothers, cleaving new paths surrounded by radicalism and abstruseness. "There is a general Islamic awakening, no doubt about it. But it is also resurrecting old differences which are consuming its strengths to no avail," he said to his brother Hakim. However, Hakim had other priorities and, despite his personal feelings, saw what befell the regime on June 5 as an absolute catastrophe; the nation was moving into uncharted territory. As the days went by, God granted Salim fatherhood, material abundance, and satisfaction on the day of victory. Yet none of this jostled from his heart his deeply rooted belief in, and eternal dream of, the divine perfect city. He swept Hadiya along in his forceful current until she said, "I was lost and you showed me the right way. Praise be to God."

Salim became a propagandist writer for the Muslim Brotherhood's magazine and, like the rest of the group, was filled with rage at Sadat's reckless venture to make peace with Israel. He reverted once more to vehement anger and rebellion, and when the September 1981 rulings were issued he was thrown back in jail. When Sadat was assassinated he said, "It's a divine punishment for an infidel government."

He could breathe freely in the new climate but had lost confidence in everything except his dream. It was for this that he worked and lived.

Samira Amr Aziz

She was Amr's fourth child and second only to Matariya in beauty. As she played on the roof and beneath the walnut trees in the square and studied at Qur'an school, her serious personality, calm nature, and brilliant mind crystallized. She seldom got involved in quarrels with her siblings and when violence flared up would withdraw into a corner, content to watch what she would later be summoned to bear witness to. Though more beautiful, she resembled her mother in general appearance—except for her height, at which Radia greatly marveled. In contrast to her sisters, she retained the principles of reading and writing that she learned at Qur'an school and nurtured them diligently, so she was the only one to regularly read newspapers and magazines as an adult. On visits to the Murakibi family at the mansion on Khayrat Square and the Dawud family in East Abbasiya, she made a mental note of the elegant setup, table manners, rhythm of conversation, and beautiful style and tried to adopt and emulate them as far as means and circumstances allowed. Mahmud Bey would joke in his crude manner, "You're a peasant family, but there is a European girl in your midst!"

She entered adolescence but did not have to dream secretly of romance for long, for a friend of her brother Amer called Hussein Qabil, who owned an antique shop in Khan al-Khalili, came and asked for her hand. He had kept her brother company up to the baccalaureate then taken over from his father when he died. Despite his youth, his manly features catapulted him into manhood early. He had a huge body, a large head, and sharp eyes, and was generous and very well-off. Unlike Sadriya and Matariya, Samira was wedded to her husband in an outer suburb, in one of the apartments of a new building on Ibn Khaldun Street. This suited her very well for she met many Jewish families, learned how to play the piano, and raised a puppy called Lolli that she would take with her on walks around al-Zahir Baybars Garden. When Amr heard about this he said, both protesting and accepting the situation, "It's God's will. There is no power or strength but in God."

Hussein Qabil was wealthy and generous, so fountains of luxury burst forth in his house and Samira could gratify her hidden longing for style and elegant living. Her happiness was compounded by her husband's good company and manners, and the fact that he addressed her as "Samira Hanem" in front of others while she called him "Hussein Bey." Sincere patriotism and deep piety filled the man's heart and he spread them to everyone around him, and so the 1919 Revolution penetrated Samira's heart in a way it did not the hearts of her sisters. Similarly, her piety was the most sound of the young women because she was the least influenced by Radia's mysteries. She gave birth to Badriya, Safa, Hakim, Faruq, Hanuma, and Salim, all of whom enjoyed a generous share of beauty and intelligence. The parents worked together to bring them up well in an atmosphere of religion and principle. From the first day she said to Hussein Qabil, "We will educate the girls along with the boys." He agreed enthusiastically.

Samira's glow was enough to stir jealousy among the Murakibi and Dawud families. Yet her life was not devoid of great sorrow, for she lost Badriya and Hakim and his family, and anxiety about Salim broke her heart at various points in her life. Astonishingly, she met these calamities with a strong, patient, and faithful will and was able to confront and endure them. But the forbearance with which she endured her sorrow also made her vulnerable to accusations of coldness.

"You should believe in amulets, spells, incense, and tombs. There is no knowledge but that of the forefathers," Radia said to her. Samira secretly asked herself whether it was these that had protected Sadriya and Matariya from calamities.

Death came and Hussein Qabil died a year after Salim was born, four years after her own father's death. He left her nothing except a depository of antiques. She sold them as the need arose and lived on the proceeds. He died just as his children were moving from secondary school to university.

"What's left for you now, Samira?" Radia asked.

"A depository of antiques," she replied.

"No, you still have the Creator of heaven and earth," said her mother.

Shin

Shazli Muhammad Ibrahim

THE SECOND SON OF MATARIYA and Muhammad Ibrahim, he was born and grew up in his parents' house in Watawit. He was good looking, but less so than his deceased brother, Ahmad. He took his brother's place as his uncle Qasim's playmate but did not achieve the same legendary status. From childhood, he frequented the house of his grandfather Amr and the families of Surur, al-Murakibi, and Dawud and continued to do so throughout his life, borrowing his love of people and socializing from his mother. From childhood too, attributes that would accompany him through life manifested: amiability, a penchant for fun, hunger for knowledge, love of girls, and all-round success in all of these, though his academic achievements were only average. His love of knowledge probably came from his father and it prospered with the books and magazines he procured for himself. Besides his relatives, he made friends with the leading thinkers of the day, who woke him from slumber and inflamed him with questions that would dog him all his life. Despite his burgeoning humanism, he inclined to mathematics so entered the faculty of science, then became a teacher like his father, remaining in Cairo thanks to the intercession of the Murakibi and Dawud families. He proceeded through life concerned with his culture and oblivious to the future until his father said to him, "You're a teacher. The teaching profession is traditional. You should start thinking about marriage."

"There are lots of girls in the family—your aunts' daughters and our uncle's daughter, Zayna," said Matariya.

He had casually courted a number of girls but did not have genuine feelings for any of them.

"I'll marry as it suits me," he said.

"A teacher must maintain a good reputation," his father cautioned.

"A 'good reputation'?" He was going through a period when he questioned the meaning of everything, even a "good reputation." Whenever he was alone he would ask himself the question: Who am I? His thirst to define his relationship to existence was obsessive and consuming. He never stopped debating with people, especially those in whom he recognized a taste for it, like his cousin Hakim and other young men in the families of al-Murakibi, Dawud, and Surur. Later he ventured to have audiences with Taha Hussein, al-Aqqad, al-Mazini, Haykal, Salama Musa, and Shaykh Mustafa Abd al-Raziq. He did not reject religion but sought to base himself in reason as far as possible. Every day he had a new concern. He would even hold discussions and confide in his uncle Qasim and interrogate relatives in their graves on cemetery festivals.

When his grandfather Amr was carried to bed breathing his last, a nurse called Suhayr was brought to administer an injection. Shazli fell in love with her despite the grief that reigned. He helped her heat some water while his uncle Amer's wife, Iffat, quietly observed them with a sly, wicked look in her eyes. As the 1940s approached, their love cemented. He realized he was more serious than he had imagined this time and announced his wish to marry. Matariya said frankly, "Your face is handsome but your taste is appalling!"

He responded to the rebuke with a laugh.

"Her roots are lowly and her appearance is commonplace," Matariya went on.

"Prepare for the wedding," he said to her.

Muhammad Ibrahim accepted the situation unperturbed and Matariya did not dare to anger her son beyond what she had said already. Shazli selected an apartment in a new building on Abu Khuda Street and embarked on a life of love and matrimony. Suhayr gave up her job and devoted herself to married life. She proved elegant and agreeable and soon won her mother-in-law's acceptance. Shazli was unlucky with his children; five died in infancy and the only one to live, Muhammad, became an army officer and was martyred in the Tripartite Aggression. Shazli spent his life searching for himself. He would read, debate, and question, only to hit a wall of skepticism and begin the game again. He was not interested in politics, except insofar as events that invited reflection and understanding, and so did not fall under the magic of the Wafd but followed the ups and downs of the July Revolution as one might an emotive film in the cinema. Yet he was disconsolate to lose Muhammad and never recovered from his grief. "Neither of us was created for pure happiness," he once said to his sister, Amana. He found some solace in loving her children. He was fearful of the severity and vehemence of his cousin Salim, his niece Hadiya's husband, and found neither enjoyment nor pleasure in his conversation. Salim said to him, "Your confusion is a foreign import. It shouldn't trouble a Muslim."

He continued to love Qasim in spite of what happened to him. He sometimes went with him to the Misri Club, where they were flooded by memories of their fathers and grandfathers. As a teacher, he would observe the up-and-coming generations in dismay. He once said to himself: People only care about a morsel of bread and emigrating, so what is the use of suffering?

Shakir Amer Amr

He was born and grew up in Bayn al-Ganayin, a street lined with modern houses and fields of vegetables and henna bushes extending east and west. He was the first child of Amer and Iffat, and the grandson of Amr Effendi and Abd al-Azim Pasha Dawud. The income from his father's salary and private lessons and the small elegant house with a grape trellis, guava tree, and clove bushes in the back garden that his mother owned meant the family enjoyed a comfortable lifestyle, just as it abundantly granted him, the eldest child, a smart appearance and not unreasonable pampering. Though sport was his forte he also achieved good results at school. When his brothers, Qadri and Fayyid, entered the world, sibling rivalry played its part, including fights and a contest with the parents, but the family was nevertheless regarded as cohesive and harmonious. The parents' mutual love emitted pure breezes that promoted an atmosphere of peace and spread affection. The father's integrity was as obvious as the mother's endeavors to control. Shakir loved his grandparents Amr and Radia, and always displayed respect for Radia's mysteries. Likewise, he loved his grandparents Abd al-Azim Pasha Dawud and Farida Hanem Husam. He took on the Dawud family's customary contempt for the Murakibis, which intensified after Shakira became his mother, Iffat's, sister-in-law. He grew up loyal to his family and his inner self more than to the nation or any political party. This was something he inherited from his mother, who was uninterested because of her upbringing, though on formal occasions would profess her father's loyalty to Adli. As for Shakir's own father, nothing remained of his Wafdism in the family home except a faint sentiment he kept hidden and which thus made no impression on the children.

Shakir enrolled in the faculty of medicine and plunged into

his first serious emotional experience when he fell in love with Safa, his aunt Samira's daughter. News of their romance reached his mother, Iffat, and she flew into a frenzy. There was nothing essentially wrong with Safa—she was a beautiful medical student and one of the family. However, despite a good relationship with them, Iffat considered her cousin Amr's family beneath her; her son's bride should rank higher on the social scale. Her anger was aroused and she did not conceal it. She made her feelings known to Samira and Amr's families and offense was taken. At the same time, Shakir himself did not display any real opposition to his mother. Samira thus advised her daughter to sever relations with her cousin. The young girl was angry for her family honor and ended the relationship once she was convinced he was not serious about it. Shakir did not suffer particularly, though was rather annoyed at his mother. He graduated a doctor and, with his uncle Doctor Lutfi Pasha Abd al-Azim's help, was appointed to a post in the ministry of health's laboratories, then opened a clinic specializing in blood diseases a few years later. His mother began planning how to realize her dream of a marriage she judged to be suitable for her son. He was a frequent patron of the nightclubs along Pyramids Road and fell for a Hungarian dancer. He rented an apartment for her near the Pyramids and the relationship developed into genuine love, so he married her in secret. He did not dare reveal the truth directly to his mother, but he did tell his father. Iffat was stunned. She raised a storm that everyone heard about, and there was much gloating. The doctor moved to his new apartment and it looked like he would be cut off from the family. "Don't grudge your son. Marriage is fate in the end," Radia said to Iffat.

As time passed limited relations resumed. The July Revolution came and society was turned on its head. The Dawud family was stripped of its pasha rank and the value of doctors and judges diminished. Shakir's hatred of the new era made him a nervous wreck. He made plans to emigrate and seized the opportunity to attend a medicine conference in Chicago. He left for the United States and took up residence there, severing relations with both his nation and his family. He returned in the middle of the 1980s accompanied by his wife and children. He visited his parents, siblings, and grandmother Radia as a foreign guest, then quickly returned to his adopted country.

Shakira Mahmud Ata al-Murakibi

Her eyes opened onto the mansion on Khayrat Square with its furniture, objets d'art, and lush garden. She had the misfortune of inheriting her most important features from her father, Mahmud Bey, with no sign of the beauty and charm her mother, Nazli Hanem, possessed. She was of medium build, had a large head and coarse features, was stubborn to the extreme in her decisions, zealous in her views, and could not be moved from a sentiment. She was also deeply pious, with firm morals and urbane, refined manners. Had she been otherwise, her father would not have married her to Hamid Amr to safeguard her from opportunists. Despite the vast difference between their two families, no one in Amr's house was enthusiastic about the marriage except Amr himself; from the moment the engagement was announced they referred to her as "Shakira Bey Ata."

Shakira loyally loved her young husband from the first day and was completely ready to open her heart to everyone in his family. True, she was not unaware that his common tastes, customs, and conduct were a long way from her refined and urbane upbringing, but she told herself, "Everything can change!" She noticed too that his affection for her was a passing whim and that the first signs of boredom appeared during the honeymoon itself. This realization hit her like a bolt of lightning and caused her immense pain, its poison piercing her love and pride. She did not keep secrets from her mother. "These things will pass. Be subtle and smart," said Nazli Hanem, speaking to her as a lady of experience and concealing the anxiety in her heart. She also said, "He comes from a common environment and because he is a policeman he only ever deals with good-for-nothings."

Hamid was heedful of his father-in-law's power and of living among his relations, so he would not raise his voice, but instead made his words gentle yet simultaneously hurtful. Once, when Shakira was angry, she said to him, "Most people don't know a blessing until it's gone."

He guffawed scornfully and replied, "Me marrying you is a blessing. You're absolutely right!"

"Then why did you agree?"

"Marriage is fate."

"And ambition and greed too!"

Thus began a struggle that would go on for years and end in divorce. It grew gradually more heated and one day she screamed at him, "You exude filth!"

"Didn't they tell you about your grandfather, the pantofle seller?" he asked sarcastically.

Yet despite her fury and stubbornness, Shakira did not lack judgment, so the secrets of her wretched marriage remained concealed within the narrowest confines. Even Nazli Hanem did not know the full details. Indeed, in spite of everything, Shakira's love for her husband did not dry up until after her father's death. She gave birth to Wahida and Salih and dearly hoped he would change with time, but it was no use. Relations with his family fared no better; she had thought Radia eccentric before she married and now decided she was insane. The two women hated one another with a passion despite Radia and Nazli's close friendship.

"Be careful not to provoke your mother-in-law. She fraternizes with the jinn," said Nazli.

"I depend on God alone," Shakira replied.

She and Amer's wife, Iffat, also detested one another, compounding the envy and aversion between Ata and Dawud's families. When the older generation passed away, Hamid could breathe freely. His wrath was unleashed in an atmosphere free of constraints and the matter ended in divorce. Shakira began to despise Hamid and his family deeply and her rage never subsided. She continued to curse and cut him to pieces for the rest of her life. In her loneliness religion claimed her. She performed the hajj more than once and was as bent on the rituals of prayer, fasting, and alms-giving as she was on cursing her enemies and damning them in this world and the next.

Shahira Mu'awiya al-Qalyubi

She was the second daughter of Shaykh Mu'awiya and Galila al-Tarabishi. She was born and grew up in the old family house in Suq al-Zalat in Bab al-Sha'riya. The hallway of the house was her playground, between the stove, well, and family sofa, where she, Radia, Sadiqa, and Baligh would congregate. There sounded her father, the shaykh's, exhortations, and there circulated Galila's mysteries of times past. From the beginning, Shahira showed no interest in religion or religious duties. Yet she eagerly embraced popular heritage and would add to it from her abundant imagination. In body and face she resembled Radia, though she was fairer, remarkably blunt and impudent, and eccentric to the point of insanity. Two years after her father died, one of his students, a Qur'an reciter with a sweet voice, nice appearance, and ample means, sought her hand in marriage. She was wedded to him in his house in Bab al-Bahr, not far from the family residence. She gave birth to a fine-looking son, whom his father called Abduh because he thought the name of the man whose voice he adored, Abduh al-Hamuli, would be a good omen. The marriage prospered in spite of Shahira's irascibility and impudence. "It's the spice of married life," the husband, Shaykh Ali Bilal, would joke.

Shaykh Ali Bilal made friends with Amr Effendi and his family, and whenever he visited the house on Bayt al-Qadi Square, Amr would ask him to bless it with one of his recitations. Thus, he would sit cross-legged in the reception room after supper, drinking coffee, and recite something easy from the Qur'an in his sweet voice. He was impelled by his voice and friends to recite eulogies to the Prophet at festivals. His livelihood grew and his admirers multiplied. Before long he was invited to enliven weddings with his panegyrics. Amidst the festive atmosphere and pleasant evenings, he got into the habit of smoking hashish. Eventually one of the composers suggested he try singing, foreseeing a rosy future in it for him. The shaykh met the invitation with a merry heart. He saw nothing wrong in abandoning the holy suras of the Qur'an to sing, "Don't Speak to Me, Papa Is Coming," "Draw the Curtains So the Neighbors Can't See," and "Yummy Scrummy Fried Fish," and was remarkably successful in so doing. He made recordings, which were circulated in the market, and people started talking about him. Amr clapped his hands together. "What a comedown!"

The temptations of the new milieu made Shahira anxious about her position as wife. "You were a blessed shaykh when I married you," she said. "Now you're a chanteuse!"

The man was intoxicated by his success and became the organizer of many a hashish gathering. He was soon drinking heavily and the house would be filled with horrid trenchant fumes at the end of the night, reminding Shahira of the tragedy of her brother, Baligh. The sound of her upbraiding and scalding him with her vicious tongue would drown the dawn muezzin. Then reports of him flirting with singers reached her ears. She pounced on him with a savagery that flung open the gates of hell upon him and he made up his mind to divorce her. But one night, before he could put his decision into action, he overdid the drinking and singing and had a heart attack. He died among friends, plucking the strings on his lute.

Shahira performed the rituals of mourning without emotion. She leased the house and the shop below and returned with Abduh to the old house to share her loneliness with her mother, Galila. "Let Abduh be your eye's delight," said Radia. But Abduh was snatched away in a fever, as though in a dream. By this time his mother was already known as Umm Abduh about the quarter, and the eponym would stick for the rest of her life. She became passionate about breeding cats and dedicated her time to looking after them until they filled the gap in her life and crowded the old house. She started to believe she could under-stand their language and the spirits that inhabited their bodies, and that through them she was in touch with the Unknown. She found her best friend in Radia. Whenever they met up, whether in Bayt al-Qadi or Suq al-Zalat, a curious session invariably ensued during which they would exchange anecdotes about the realm of the jinn, the Unknown, and the offspring of mysteries. In such things they were of one heart and one mind, despite Radia's misgivings and suspicion that Shahira begrudged her her children and happy marriage. Shahira was famous in Suq al-Zalat for her inscrutable, fearful personality and impudent tongue. She was not known to perform any religious duties and would prepare her meal at sunset in Ramadan saying, "People don't need religious duties to bring them closer to God." After her mother died she was wholly immersed in solitude, sub-merged to the top of her gray head in a world of cats. Her brother, Baligh, saw to her upkeep. He would invite her to visit his sublime mansion, but she hated his wife for no real reason, and only ever left her cats to visit Sidi al-Sha'rani or Radia. She fell victim to the cholera epidemic of 1947 and moved to the fever hospital after instructing a neighbor to go to Radia for the cats' care. She died in hospital, leaving some forty cats behind. Radia's sons and daughters mourned the aunt whom they had laughed at in life.

Ṣad

Salih Hamid Amr

HE GREW UP IN THE MANSION ON KHAYRAT SQUARE in the wing set aside for Hamid and Shakira. He and his sister, Wahida, represented the first generation of grandchildren in the Murakibi family and, consequently, enjoyed special deference from their grandparents and maternal aunts and uncles. The big garden was his playground and dream; he loved it in spring, with its abundant medley of pure fragrances, and he loved it in winter, when it was cleansed by the water of precious rains. He was closer to his mother than his father, whose time was taken up with work, and became even more so each time he perceived signs of the ordeal the man put her through. He was strong bodied like his father and good looking like his grandfather, but his mother gave him a pious, aristocratic, and urbane upbringing so he grew into a man of integrity and religious principles. He was also headstrong like his mother, which led some to believe him ignorant, which was far from the truth. The impression was intensified by the harsh way in which he judged people by the Qur'an and Sunna, intolerant and inflexible. His father was probably his first victim despite the fact that the man loved him dearly. He loved his father too, but considered him vulgar and placed him in the same bracket as sinners and good-for-nothings while granting him his full due of reverence and loyalty. Hamid instinctively grasped his position and complained about it to his brother, Amer. "Shakira has brought them up to dislike me."

Thus, Amer said to him one day, "You're a good man, Salih. Don't forget to respect your father."

"I never neglect my duty to my father," he replied.

"Perhaps he isn't content with formalities."

"He abuses Mama, Uncle," he said with absolute frankness.

He was similar in temperament to his cousin Salim, but with one difference; Salim combined emotion with action, whereas he would say to himself: The heart's enough; it's still conviction. Thus, he loved the Muslim Brothers without joining the organization and pledged loyalty, as a Murakibi, to the Crown just as he lent money to all the parties. As a result of the eternal struggle between his parents he generally shunned his father's relatives— the families of Amr and Surur—and despised the Dawud family. Like his mother, he believed his grandmother Radia was quite simply mad. Because he continued to achieve in school Hamid said to him, "You should study medicine. You're right for it."

"No. Agriculture. You have land you can farm afterward," said Shakira.

He preferred his mother's idea and Hamid privately cursed the two of them. After graduation he traveled to Beni Suef, determined to make a modern farm out of the land his mother inherited when his tyrant grandfather died. He married a woman called Galfadan, a relative of his grandmother Nazli Hanem, and with high hopes dedicated himself to working on the land. He bred calves and set up a beehive to produce honey. He dressed in the clothes of a country nobleman and only wore a suit when he visited Cairo. His heart was hostile to the July Revolution, even though it did not harm him personally and two of his uncles, Abduh and Mahir, were among its men. In the period of the infitah, his livelihood increased, his family expanded and he remained loyal to his principles. His indignation at his father intensified after the man divorced his mother and married a second time, but he was genuinely sad when he died. He grew accustomed to country life. He loved it and was passionate about his work and success, and began to refer to Cairo as "The City of Pain."

Sadriya Amr Aziz

She was rightly said to be a gift in Amr's family. Like the others, she was born and grew up in the old house on Bayt al-Qadi Square. Her skin was a deep shade of brown and she was small with a slender, well-shaped body and pleasant features. She was received with subdued joy for she disappointed hopes of a male child. As the eldest, she took on a motherly role toward her brothers and sisters from childhood. She was her mother's confidante and heiress to her heritage, but she was not without a measure of conventional religion, and her domestic skills, from cooking to cleaning and needlework, were exemplary. She was sent to Qur'an school and learned how to read and write but reverted to illiteracy when they were not put to use. She worked and sang unceasingly even though she was not endowed with a particularly good voice. You would find her in the kitchen helping her mother or laboring in her mother's place, sitting at the sewing machine, or on the roof checking on the chickens and rabbits. When the house crowded with Amer, Matariya, Samira, Habiba, Hamid, and Qasim, she played deputy to her mother while joining in the games, gaiety, shouting, and battles, and excelling all round. She obtained a status enjoyed by no one else, which she maintained for the rest of her life. She shared everyone's worries, despite the burden of her own, and had total faith in her mother, whom she saw as a miracle worker.

She had barely turned fifteen when a country nobleman from Upper Egypt called Hamada al-Qinawi came forward to ask for her hand and a dream she had entertained since the age of ten came true. Her departure represented the first farewell and first wedding celebration in the family. Hamada was an acquaintance of Amr's. He adored Cairo, so when his father died he had moved there with his mother and leased his thirty feddans of land to an uncle in Qina. Rashwana, Radia, and Surur's wife, Zaynab, visited the man's house in Darb al-Qazzazin.

"Hamada's mother is devout. No religious duty is above her," Rashwana said to her brother Amr.

At a gathering in Amr's house attended by Amr, Surur, and Mahmud Bey Ata, Surur Effendi said, "The groom is unemployed and has no skills. That's bad."

"He has thirty feddans," said Amr.

"Even so, he is barely literate," replied Surur with unfounded conceit.

"A man's value is in his money," said Mahmud Ata.

"He is from a good traditional family," said Amr.

From what she could see through the gap in the mashrabiya Sadriya was pleased with Hamada's appearance; he was tall and strong, smartly dressed in a jubbah and caftan, and had manly features. She was wedded to him in a house in Khan Ga'far that he rented from the dimwitted pastry man. Mahmud Ata furnished the reception room, Ahmad Bey gave jewelry and clothes, and Abd al-Azim Dawud provided the wedding dress. Sadriya began her married life with Hamada resting on her mother's instructions, her blessings, and superior skills as a mistress of the house. Hamada represented a complex problem. They were mutually affectionate and each felt a strong need for the other, but Sadriya was naturally sensitive and irascible and very stubborn while her husband was a narrow-minded chatterbox who loved glory and authority. His unlimited spare time left him free to interfere in things whether or not they concerned him. She was not accustomed to a man snoring away until noon, waking up, and interrupting her housework to talk endlessly about his family, its merits, and his own illusory virtues, followed by foolish comments on her work, about which he understood nothing. He knew his religion only by name and did not pray or fast. Barely a night went by when he did not stay up late at the Parisienne, drinking wine and dining on appetizers. Yet they did not shun marital relations or children, and so she gave birth to Nihad, Aql, Warda, and Dalal. Nor did they refrain from futile debates, hence he would boast about his family of landowners and she would in turn extol the families of Ata and Dawud and Shaykh Mu'awiya, the hero of the Urabi Revolution. The discussion would sometimes become heated and they would exchange cruel insults. She strove to hide the steam from the cooking pot under a tight lid and solve her problems herself without involving her family. But Radia perceived what was going on through her own intuition as well as from the man's excruciating chatter. "A wife has to be a doctor," she said to her daughter.

"You must visit the relevant tombs," said Sadriya.

"What is the point in visiting tombs for this? The best remedy is to cut off his tongue!" said Radia.

The truth was that it was not just Hamada's wife who suffered from his irritating chatter; on visits he would inflict it on the families of Amr, Surur, al-Murakibi, and Dawud until it became a joke among the relatives. It became clear that her husband's eyes knew no shame and followed every pretty girl who passed by. Sadriya grew increasingly uneasy.

"Have you no shame?" she asked him disapprovingly.

"There's no harm in looking," he scoffed.

But she caught gestures between him and the beautiful widow who lived in the house opposite. A fire ignited inside her and blew the sleep from her eyes. She stayed awake until the time he usually came home from an evening at the Parisienne then left the house and went out into the street, wrapped in the darkness, with a bucket of water in her hand. Hamada approached, cleaving his way through the pitch-dark night. She felt the door of the widow's house open and the woman's blurred outline appeared dimly in the doorway. The man paused and turned toward it. Sadriya hurried into the middle of the road and hurled the water at the woman in the doorway, who screamed and tumbled backward into the house. Hamada was startled. He looked in Sadriya's direction, "Who are you?"

"Get home, you shameless creature!" she shouted enraged.

He was staggering that night. He entered the house in silence then shouted angrily, "I'll show you how savage I can be when I need to."

But in his drunkenness he was overcome by laughter. He collapsed onto the sofa saying, "You're a madwoman like your mother!"

She quarreled with him for a while, then they reverted to friendly relations and bickering, although the matter was not laid entirely to rest until he fell ill. He developed high blood pressure that affected his heart and he had to give up drinking. A general apathy came over him, which in certain guises took on the appearance of wisdom. Then came sorrow; Sadriya lost her daughter, Warda, in the prime of youth, and then lost her father and her sister Matariya. Finally, Hamada died on a visit to his family in Qina. Sadriya remained in Khan Ga'far, refusing to move to her son Aql's house despite his strong devotion to her. When Radia sensed her health was deteriorating she said to Sadriya, "I want you by my side to close my eyes. . . ." Thus, she shut up her house and returned to the house of her birth to be beside her mother, who favored her above everyone. Radia was over a hundred years old and Sadriya was herself approaching ninety, although she was in full possession of her strength and still active. The final days passed in a turmoil of memories; her mother recalled songs she had sung in the last quarter of the nineteenth century then passed away. Sadriya closed her eyes, wanting to cry but unable to.

Sadiqa Mu'awiya al-Qalyubi

The third daughter of Shaykh Mu'awiya and Galila al-Tarabishi, she was born in the old house in Suq al-Zalat half a year after the shaykh was put in prison. She was more beautiful than her two sisters, Radia and Shahira. Indeed, with her fair complexion, rosy cheeks, symmetrical features, ample black hair, and succulent slender body she was an unrivaled beauty in the quarter. In the family she was surpassed only by Amr and Radia's daughter Matariya, who shared the same roots but was more light-hearted and urbane. She was the only one not to claim her portion of the shaykh's religious upbringing and grew up the pure fruit of Galila's heritage. She was kind toward others and loved singing, justified by a fine voice. Because of her beauty and geniality, she enjoyed the greatest share of Radia's children's affection.

A few years after her father's death and one year after Shahira married, a Syrian dentist resident in the quarter presented himself and she was wedded to him. They moved into a new building in Faggala. It was not long before disaster struck; her husband died before she conceived and she herself contracted tuberculosis. She returned to Galila's arms, seeking warmth and healing. The family's hearts were shaken by her bad luck. Her beauty withered and her life was transformed. Pain assailed her and there was no hope of recovery. She felt she was sinking into the abyss. She grew tired of the desperation, the suffering, the insomnia, the coughing, and in a moment of dark despair threw herself into the well. Galila screamed and caring neighbors rushed to her side. They extricated her on the point of death. She suffered hours of agony through a long feverish night, surrounded by her mother and sisters, Radia and Shahira, the doorway choked with male relatives and neighbors. After an excruciating struggle she passed away shortly before dawn, at the height of youth, despair, and suffering.

Galila grieved for a long time. She ordered a firm wooden lid to be placed over the well and that it never be used again. She dreamed about her daughter from time to time and once said to Radia, "On the night of Sidi al-Sha'rani I saw Sadiqa standing on a white cloud near the well. Her face was bright and she was smiling."

Radia had deep faith in her mother. "Did she speak to you, Mama?" she asked.

"I asked her how she was and she told me that God had forgiven her for taking her life. She told me this to put my heart at rest," Galila replied.

"Praise God, the Merciful and Compassionate," cried Radia.

"I saw her at her most beautiful, like in the old days," said Galila.

Safa Hussein Qabil

She was the second child of Samira and Hussein Qabil. She was born and grew up in the house on Ibn Khaldun Street. She suckled in her wholesome, affluent cradle under the protective shade of days of glory and well-being and the lush greenery of al-Zahir Baybars Garden. Samira's children were good looking, healthy, and successful, but Safa was the most beautiful and joyful of all. How she played with and danced for her grandmother Radia and exuded pure warmth everywhere she went. She grew up modest and forbearing and worshiped life above the various principles of her brothers and sisters. Hussein Qabil adored her; to him she was a treasure more beautiful than any he bought or sold. She did well at school and enrolled in the English language department at the faculty of arts. Hussein Qabil died, leaving a deep wound in her heart. She could feel her mother's pain as she adjusted the family to a different standard of living, and a darkness blacker than the darkness of war and air raids settled over her. On her rounds she met her young male relatives from the families of Surur, al-Murakibi, and Dawud but it was Shakir, her uncle Amer's son, who cast the net of interest and admiration over her. He was a medical student and they were able to meet often away from family traditions. Her heart was weaned in his hands and she believed he was the man of the happy future she anticipated. She noticed he was keen to shroud their relationship in secrecy but did not grasp the significance. "Who are you afraid of?" she asked him one day.

"Mama!" he replied bluntly, annoyed.

She was surprised at him and his mother and surmised he was not the man he ought to be. One day she returned from college and found her mother dejected and frowning. Knowing the strength of her mother's restraint she realized something was wrong. "Your uncle's wife, Iffat!" Samira said indignantly.

Her heart contracted and she felt her hope disappear.

"She told me categorically that I must keep you away from her son," Samira said.

"But I'm not pursuing him," she cried angrily.

"Close the door with latch and key," Samira said distressed.

There was no way out. No escape from the pain. But why?

"They look down on us," Samira went on. "It was the same for your aunt Matariya before."

"How do they see themselves?" she asked furiously.

"That's nothing to do with us. I want to trust you. . . ."

"You can trust me completely," she said disgusted.

She drank pain and humiliation. However, she had inherited some of her mother's unique personality traits, namely the ability to withstand calamity, and the relationship was severed in disdain.

She graduated and was appointed as a translator in the university administration—thanks to the good offices of senior men on her mother's side. She caught the attention of the assistant secretary and he asked to marry her. The man was about twenty years older than her but enjoyed high rank and a good income. She weighed up the offer and decided it was perfectly suited to her circumstances; she realized too that she was more "practical" than she had thought. She was married to Sabri Bey al-Qadi in his villa in al-Qubba Gardens. Her new existence accorded her the life of plenty, doting and generous husband, and motherhood of two sons—Ali and Amr—that she desired. The July Revolution played as it liked with her family, and so her brother Hakim prospered while Salim perished. It was her good fortune that Sabri al-Qadi was related to an important officer so was quickly promoted and appointed to the post of head clerk of the ministry of culture. He was pensioned off in old age but continued to encourage her until she became a director general. She supervised Ali and Amr's education until they entered the diplomatic service. Thus, this branch shone in the diamond era of bureaucracy and was spared the evil of the storms.

ʿAyn

Amer Amr Aziz

THE FIRST GIFT FROM THE UNKNOWN to flood Amr and Radia's hearts with joy, satisfaction, and pride, Amer confirmed the conviction held in Bayt al-Qadi Square that a boy is better than a girl. He came resplendent with a handsome face that borrowed the best of Radia's features—a straight nose, high forehead, and the fine facial symmetry for which Samira would later be known. His calm nature, piety, and impulse to lead and protect came from his father. How often he would assemble his brothers and sisters on the roof to play at being the Qur'an school shaykh, wielding in his hand a stick that timidity and kindness prevented him using. He grew into a smart and elegant young man who would stroll about the city quarters smiling and musing and sit cross-legged before al-Hussein's tomb in fervent prayer. He was always good at making friends with neighbors of his own class and higher ones, and scoundrels could never provoke him. He was also a favorite at the mansion on Khayrat Square and with the Dawud family. He did well at school, excelling in science and mathematics and, thanks to eminent relatives, was granted a remission of fees. Thus, his father was relieved of a burden he could not bear while embroiled in arranging the marriages of Sadriya, Matariya, and Samira. From childhood, Amer and Abd al-Azim Pasha Dawud's daughter Iffat were drawn to one another. It began on the roof in the shade of the hanging washing and, with passing days and visits, developed into love and hope for the future. This all took place in secret, but exuded its scent like a rose. Love was the first thing to get the better of the arrogant girl who saw her family as superior, as though God had created no one but them for nobility.

"We've educated our children in European schools to make them suitable for one of the family's doctors or public prosecutors," Farida Hanem Husam said to Abd al-Azim.

"Amr's my cousin. There's no one more upright than him," said the pasha.

The hanem shared his sentiments. She loved Radia and was particularly fond of Amer so she soon came round. Amr and Radia were delighted. Amr was proud and boastful of his grand relatives and considered a marriage connection with them a great accomplishment. Mahmud Ata Bey had been considering Amer as a husband for Shakira and when the young man fell into the hands of his rival he said to Amr, "Hamid can be Shakira's." With this Amr's happiness was complete, exposing him to his brother, Surur's, reproach. Surur blamed him for ignoring his daughters, but Amr defended his position using the beauty of Surur's daughters, who need not fear being left behind, and the poverty of his own children who needed support, as excuses.

"They wouldn't give you a son," Surur said bitterly.

Amr was hurt but in his modesty simply replied, "Praise God. A man knows his place."

Surur hid his anger. "Brother, you've become a dervish. You never get angry."

Amer wanted to enter the faculty of medicine resting on his talent for science, so that he might be "suitable" for Iffat in the full sense of the word. But his father chose the teachers college because it was free of charge.

"It's impossible to get a scholarship into medical school. The eye sees but the hand can't provide," he told his beloved son.

Amer was a model of obedience and accepted truths however bitter. He said to his father, feigning approval, "The teachers college is excellent at any rate."

Iffat and her family were forbearing. Iffat told herself a teacher she loved was better than a doctor she didn't. Amer digested his harsh disappointment and proceeded on his path crowned with success and satisfaction. He worshiped the 1919 Revolution along with the rest of his family, took part in the demonstrations, and welcomed Sa'd with an open heart. He was in his final year at the time and working life soon took him away from the immediate action. The marriage was arranged for the following year. He became a guest in his family, in whose hearts he left nothing but goodwill, with the exception of a certain enmity between him and his brother Hamid on account of the latter's rebellious nature and unruly behavior. How many incantations and amulets Radia expended to drive the evil spirit away from the two of them! However, as soon as they began their working lives the murk cleared. Abd al-Azim Dawud built a house for his daughter in Bayn al-Ganayin. He fitted it with electricity, a water supply, drains, and a small garden at the back, and Amer and his Europhile wife moved in to begin a long and happy married life.

The marriage shook Amr's family from the first day. It was quite clear that the new wife was of a different species to Amer's sisters as she had graduated from La Mère de Dieu, spoke several languages, was a skilled piano player, and knew all about France, its history and its religion, and almost nothing about her own country's heritage or beliefs. Moreover, she prided herself on this in spite of the spirit of nationalism unleashed with the 1919 Revolution. Her strong, overpowering personality swallowed her meek, gentle husband's and the young man did not dare remind her that fasting was a duty in Ramadan; he fasted alone and prepared his own meal before daybreak. She also dazzled him with her unintelligible conversation and skill at the piano. When Adli's supporters came out against Sa'd Zaghloul, Amer found himself a foreigner in the Dawud family. He avoided disturbing the peace in defense of his latent Wafdism and kept it to himself. Iffat had no serious interest in politics, though she went along with her father out of loyalty. "There's no comparison between the noble Adli Pasha and your Azharite leader!" she would tell her husband. But Amer would smile and spurn the quarrel.

Once Abd al-Azim Dawud asked him, "Do you really believe we can bear the burden of independence?"

"Why not?" he asked.

"We thought about full independence but we would be lost and merciless without the British Protectorate," Abd al-Azim replied.

Although close friends with Farida Hanem and an admirer of Iffat's beauty, Radia was angered by Iffat's superiority and Amer's submission.

"A man should be master of his house," she said to her son.

"Iffat fancies herself a princess," she said to Amr.

"Don't stir Amer into something that will spoil his happiness," her husband advised. Radia was won over in the end, especially after Iffat gave birth to Shakir, Qadri, and Fayyid, whom she loved with all her heart. Amer and Iffat's firm love overcame any differences and their partnership represented a rare example of happy matrimony: a marriage that knew no ennui, relapse, speculation, or jealousy.

"The secret of my brother's happiness is that he's dissolved in his wife's will. What a price to pay," said Hamid.

Surur Effendi said to his wife, Zaynab, with typical contempt and bitterness, "Hamid has married a man and Iffat has married a woman."

Amer was as successful in his career as he was in his marriage. He was the students' favorite teacher, the one who influenced them the most, and one of the few who retain for life memories of those they have taught over the generations. He profited from this, for he increased his income with private lessons and overcame a number of obstacles through the influence of certain former students. As for the zenith of his fortunes, it came after the July Revolution when two of his students found themselves in the council of leaders. Iffat abhorred the revolution because it negated her brother's pasha rank. She could not forgive it for its contempt of high-ranking professions like medicine and law. But thanks to his two students, Amer felt he was one of its men, despite the Wafdist sympathies he suppressed among the Dawud family.

Amer's children brought him no less happiness than his marriage did. They were talented and successful, although they caused their parents more trouble than they imagined through their personal behavior and politics. Then everything settled down and Amer entered a quarter century of retirement in a house that became a model of companionship in old age just as it had been one of happiness in love. He kept his health and vitality. He read newspapers and magazines, listened to music, and watched television. Because he was in good health while his wife's health declined, he did the chores and supervised the servants and cooking himself. He would play with the grandchildren or, pricked by nostalgia, would drive out to the old quarter with one of his children and visit the old house where Qasim lived, pray at al-Hussein's tomb, sit for an hour at al-Fishawi, dine at al-Dahhan then return to Bayn al-Ganayin intoxicated and joyful. He lived until he was nearly ninety, and so he rejoiced at the July glories, was burned by June 5, recovered on May 15, rejoiced once more on the resounding October 5, then was dejected on the bloody October 6. He departed the world in enviable calm, like a happy ending. He woke up one morning at the usual time and went to the kitchen to prepare tea for himself and Iffat. He returned to drink it in bed and when he finished the glass he said, "My heart doesn't feel right." He lay down on his back to rest and before long his head turned on the pillow, as though he was nodding off to sleep.

Abd al-Azim Dawud Yazid

He was the only child of Dawud Pasha and Saniya al-Warraq who lived. He grew up in Bayt al-Sayyida and received an urbane upbringing from a hanem mother and a father who was counted among the elite of his day. From childhood, he mixed with his relatives in the old quarter and was particularly fond of his cousin Amr. But he mixed with another kind of people too: the European associates of his father, who often dined and exchanged toasts at his table. He flitted between tradition and modernity, but religion played in his life only a fraction of the role it played in his close friend Amr's. He was lean, dark skinned, good looking, and had a large head, fine mind, and a lot of ambition. He did well at school, then enrolled in the faculty of law. His father had hoped to make a doctor of him, but he liked rhetoric and belles lettres and specialized in law, in keeping with other sons of eminent men. He was appointed to the public prosecutor's office without his father's intervention and from the first day claimed the respect of his superiors, the English in particular.

He was perhaps the first to choose a wife on one sighting. He caught a glimpse of Farida Husam in the family carriage and was attracted by her fair complexion and elegant features, so he found out the name of the family. Saniya al-Warraq, Radia, and Rashwana went to visit the distinguished family and reported back that Husam was a wealthy Syrian silk merchant. Farida was wedded to Abd al-Azim in a villa on Sarayat Road, bringing with her fresh beauty, wealth, and a pleasant readiness for married life. As the days passed, she gave birth to Lutfi, Ghassan, Halim, Fahima, and Iffat. Abd al-Azim excelled in his work and was interested in politics. He was a supporter of the Umma

Party and was friends with prominent men, and he believed in the Watani Party drivel. His heart blazed with enthusiasm for the 1919 Revolution, but when the front split, he inclined with heart and mind to Adli Yakan and his companions. He saw his cousin Amr's confusion and laughed uproariously.

"You're bewitched by the great buffoon."

"He's the leader of the nation and its hope," said Amr.

Amr would feel the warm bond between him and Abd al-Azim when his cousin visited him in Bayt al-Qadi. But when he went to the villa on Sarayat Road he felt lost in the "European" atmosphere that governed behavior and customs there, including Abd al-Azim Pasha's habit of whetting his appetite with two glasses of whisky and sometimes speaking to his two daughters, Fahima and Iffat, in French. Mahmud Ata al-Murakibi ingratiated himself with the pasha, keen to strengthen relations with him despite the hidden rivalry between their two families. In truth, Abd al-Azim Pasha did not particularly like the man but would exchange visits out of respect for his cousin Amr. Mahmud Bey once sought to use Abd al-Azim's influence in one of his many lawsuits but Abd al-Azim frowned and spoke frankly, "You evidently have no idea about the probity of the law." Mahmud Bey's work inspired him to believe that slogans were one thing, reality something else, so was shocked by his friend's antipathy and cursed him privately. However, he found himself on the same side as the pasha after the political schism. Seeking to make light of their differences, he said, "Allegiance to the Crown or the English, it's all the same."

"It isn't allegiance to the English, just friendship," said Abd al-Azim.

"Isn't the Crown preferable?"

"The Crown's loyalty resides with the English. We're calling for the Constitution."

"But the Constitution would deliver government to Sa'd."

"Maybe to him and them."

"He charms the people with his call for total independence. How do you stand on that?"

"The fools don't know the meaning of independence. Independence is an enormous responsibility. Where would we find the money for defense?" said the man shaking his large head. "Wouldn't it be better to leave that to the English and dedicate ourselves to reform?"

"You're right," said Mahmud Bey enthusiastically. "Zaghloul's independence could lead to another Urabi Revolution."

Abd al-Aziz's eldest son, Lutfi, fulfilled his hopes, unlike Ghassan and Halim. Nevertheless, Abd al-Azim was generally considered a lucky father. Lutfi almost went astray when he inclined to Amr's daughter, Matariya, but God was merciful, although Abd al-Azim was sad to take a stand against the daughter of his dear friend. As the days went by, he was appointed to important posts in the judiciary and was head of the High Court of Appeals when he drew his pension. His vitality enabled him to work as a lawyer until the 1950s then retire in old age. He did not sit still though; he would go each evening to the Luna Park Coffee House to play backgammon with the imperialists of his generation. By the July Revolution he had passed the age of worrying. He developed an acute burning in his prostate, was taken to hospital, and died two days later.

Abduh Mahmud Ata al-Murakibi

He was born and grew up in the mansion on Khayrat Square, the third child of Mahmud Bey and Nazli Hanem. He was characterized by good looks and nobility from childhood. He was raised in an atmosphere of grandeur and taught the principles of morality, culture, and piety at the hands of his beautiful, urbane mother. He grew up with a general aversion for socializing and though he knew his relatives from Amr, Surur, and

Rashwana's families, he did not make friends with any of them. He was fond of sports and excelled at swimming in particular. He also loved reading. He did well at school, which qualified him to enroll in the faculty of engineering, and when he graduated from there after the treaty, he joined the engineering division of the army. He began to diverge from his family's political line and did not side with the Crown like his father and uncle. Instead, like his relative Hakim Hussein Qabil, he joined the restless generation, angry at everything and searching for something new. His mother suggested he take a wife from the Mawardi family, a family of feudal lords, so he married. He rented an elegant apartment in Zamalek for his bride, but the marriage was childless and unsuccessful; its only benefit consisted in what he learned about himself. It became apparent that in spite of his wealth he could not bear parting with money; it pained him to sacrifice a piaster unnecessarily or without forethought and planning. His wife, Gulistan, adored pomp, social life, and showing off her stunning appearance, but Abduh was completely unable to give up his customs and habits. Bitterness entrapped them and made their lives an unbearable hell.

"You weren't created for partnership," his wife told him frankly.

"I absolutely agree," he replied, fumbling for his escape route.

She vacated the marital home and waited for the divorce. The issue was studied at the highest levels and Abduh found support for his position with his parents, or at least clear opposition to Gulistan's lifestyle. "I'm not in favor of divorce but in certain circumstances it's necessary and can't be avoided," said Mahmud Bey.

The divorce took place, but entailed considerable material loss with the settlement and expenses and prompted the young man to take a stand toward marriage that he would maintain for the rest of his life. He returned to his handsome room on the second floor of the mansion on Khayrat Square and devoted his energies to work and diverse reading. He, his sister Nadira, and his brother Mahir were similar in temperament, and the two brothers joined the Free Officers Movement at the appropriate time. When the July Revolution came, they found themselves in the second rank. Mahmud Bey had died by this point and they were able to save their inheritance from the grasp of the agricultural reforms. Abduh was appointed to a leading post in the army's engineering branch and, after the Setback, was entrusted with charge of a metal company as a reward for his continued loyalty to Abdel Nasser. Though he was deeply affected by the defeat of June 5, he was among those who saw the loss of land as insignificant in comparison to the country's psychological victory in preserving the leadership of Abdel Nasser and the socialist regime. He naturally regretted his brother Mahir's dismissal for allegiance to Abd al-Hakim Amer, just as he had previously regretted his older brother Hakim's pensioning off, but he could always find comfort in his mantra: "The country must come first."

He became dispensable in the time of President Sadat, so retired to his house and land. With the infitah policy he set up an engineering office with some of his colleagues and became excessively rich. He never left the mansion where he was born, nor the characteristics that had destined him for solitude. He continued to live simply despite his wealth, convinced he was amassing his money for others.

Adnan Ahmad Ata al-Murakibi

He was born and grew up in the Murakibi family mansion on Khayrat Square and learned the principles of an urbane upbringing and piety in the arms of luxury. Despite growing up with a peaceable, gentle-hearted father and a hanem mother of great dignity and morals (Fawziya Hanem, the sister of Nazli), he resembled his tyrant uncle Mahmud Bey most of all with his obstinacy and love of power. Of his generation he was the most loving to his other relatives—Amr, Surur, and Rashwana—and the most attached to the old quarter. From the beginning, he rebelled inwardly against his tyrant uncle, who imposed authority over the mansion, including his brother Ahmad's family. He had barely reached adolescence before he let it be known that he found his uncle's guardianship and monopoly on managing the land as if it was his exclusive property loathsome. He asked his mother the reason behind it but she just said, "Your father is content with things this way."

So he turned to his father and argued about it until he ruined his father's repose.

"The situation is a disgrace!" he said plainly.

He carried on until he had wrenched his father from his paradise. Events came to pass and the quarrel that would divide the respectable family into two hostile factions began; brother disowned brother, sister disowned sister, and cousin disowned cousin. Adnan challenged his uncle, who spat in his face, and exchanged blows with Hasan in the mansion's garden. A black cloud settled over the family and continued to obscure light and warmth until Ahmad Bey's death. Ahmad Bey assumed management of his land, knowing nothing of what it entailed. Losses inevitably ensued, until Adnan completed his agricultural studies and rushed to Beni Suef to take over the work from his father and save him from ruin.

In contrast to his brothers and cousins, Adnan was enamored of country girls. He fell in love with a thirty-five-year-old widow when he was not yet thirty himself and announced his wish to marry her, with no regard for his mother's anxiety. He fulfilled his wish, brought Sitt Tahani to visit the mansion, and then took her home to the farm. She gave birth to Fu'ad and Faruq then stopped having children. Whenever she grew tired of the countryside she would travel to Cairo and make life difficult for Fawziya Hanem. When the July Revolution came, Adnan—for various reasons—was the only one to whom the agriculture reform laws applied. Like his father and uncle, he pledged allegiance to the Crown and hated the revolution, though he did not say or do anything that might risk offense. Fu'ad became an excellent farmer like his father and assisted him but Faruq was a failure at school and got involved in countryside crimes until he was shot one day leaving the mosque after Friday prayers. Adnan was delighted at the Tripartite Aggression but his joy relapsed. He delighted even more on June 5, and his happiness became complete in September 1970. When Sadat assumed power his sense of loyalty to a leader returned. His heart rejoiced at Sadat's victory on October 6 and at the peace. As for the infitah policy, he considered it a gate into paradise. He farmed sheep, chickens, and eggs and made huge illusory profits. He was still not satisfied, however, so he joined the Watani Party and was elected to the People's Assembly.

Aziz Yazid al-Misri

He was born and grew up on the first floor of the house in al-Ghuriya in the shadow of Bab al-Mutawalli, the first child of Yazid al-Misri and Farga al-Sayyad. The couple produced two sons and four daughters but the daughters all died in the cradle, leaving only Aziz and Dawud. The boys enjoyed good health and grew up promising strength alongside their good looks and distinct features. They took as their playground the area between the gate and the paper supplier where their father was treasurer, on a road in Gamaliya that brimmed with people, animals, and handcarts and was surrounded by mosques and minarets. The French invasion came and went before the brothers were fully conscious, and so Napoleon Bonaparte passed them by as a radish or doum palm seller might. When Aziz was old enough, Yazid al-Misri said in his Alexandrian accent, "It's time for Qur'an school."

"No. Send him to my mother at the market," Farga al-Sayyad protested.

"It was learning to read and write that got me my job at the paper supplier," Yazid replied.

Farga believed in the market from which she came but could not change his mind. At the Shurbini Coffee Shop, Shaykh al-Qalyubi praised his decision.

"Excellent decision! Qur'an school then al-Azhar," he said.

The third friend, Ata al-Murakibi, sought refuge in silence. Ata al-Murakibi lived on the second floor of the house in al-Ghuriya with his wife, Sakina Gal'ad al-Mughawiri, and new-born daughter, Ni'ma. The three men had got to know one another at Ata al-Murakibi's shop in al-Salihiya and began meeting at the Shurbini Coffee Shop in Darb al-Ahmar to drink ginger tea and smoke hashish. Shaykh al-Qalyubi was a teacher at al-Azhar and invited the other two for dinner at his house in Suq al-Zalat several times. They saw his young son, Mu'awiya, playing between the well and stove. "Will you send him to al-Azhar after Qur'an school?" asked Ata al-Murakibi.

"God does as he wishes," said Yazid.

However, in matters of religion Yazid was, like his friend Ata, content with performing the prescribed duties and had no aspirations beyond that. Aziz began to attend Qur'an school and was soon joined by Dawud. They memorized parts of the Qur'an and learned the principles of reading, writing, and arithmetic. During this time, Dawud fell into the snare of the education program while Aziz was spared by a miracle for which he thanked God all his life. Dawud's life followed its course; meanwhile, when Aziz was old enough to work, Shaykh al-Qalyubi took steps on his behalf at the office of religious endowments and he was appointed watchman over Bayn al-Qasrayn's public fountain. He dressed in a gallabiya, pantofles, and a cotton cloak in summer, or a woolen one in winter, but swapped his turban for a tarboosh and was jokingly referred to around the quarter as Aziz Effendi, a name that stuck for life. It was settled that he would receive a millieme for every good turn. "God has granted you an important position," Yazid said to him.

His only cause for regret in those days was his brother's bad luck. His sorrow was compounded when it was decided that Dawud would be sent to France. He asked his friend, Shaykh al-Mu'awiya, who had replaced Shaykh al-Qalyubi at al-Azhar when the elder retired in old age, "What did Dawud do wrong, Shaykh Mu'awiya?"

"Not all infidel learning is heresy. Nor is living in an infidel country. Let God take care of your brother," the shaykh replied.

Aziz entered the furnace of adolescence and, despite his piety, began to stray. "We must marry him," Yazid said to Farga.

"Your friend Ata's daughter, Ni'ma, is pleasant and suitable."

The girl was wedded to Aziz at his father's house in al-Ghuriya. Two years later his friend Shaykh Mu'awiya married Galila al-Tarabishi at the house in Suq al-Zalat. Yazid al-Misri and Farga lived to see the births of Rashwana, Amr, and Surur, then Yazid died at work at the paper supplier. He was buried in the enclosure he built near the tomb of Sidi Nagm al-Din after he dreamed he saw the master inviting him to be beside him. Farga al-Sayyad joined him a year later. Significant events took place: Ni'ma's mother, Sakina, died; Ata al-Murakibi married the rich widow who lived on the top floor of the house opposite the shop and suddenly moved into a higher class. He built a mansion on Khayrat Square and purchased a farm in Beni Suef. He fathered Mahmud and Ahmad in old age and began a new life as though he was in a dream. Aziz Effendi found himself related by marriage to an important nobleman while his wife, Ni'ma, found herself the daughter of a grandee. Tongues wagged with the tale of Ata al-Murakibi, his luck, and how his rich wife melted under his wing. Yet neither Ni'ma nor her family enjoyed the benefits, with the exception of a few presents on festivals.

"If the wife dies before the husband, he and his sons will be beneficiaries and your wife will be too. But if he dies first your wife won't get anything," Shaykh Mu'awiya said to his friend Aziz.

Ata and Aziz's families exchanged visits and Amr, Surur, and Rashwana played with Mahmud and Ahmad. Aziz would run his eyes over the garden and objets d'art and mutter to himself, "Glory be to the Bestower of graces, the Giver."

"He's a boor and doesn't deserve such blessings," he said to his friend, Shaykh Mu'awiya.

"God has reasons," replied the shaykh.

Meanwhile, Dawud returned from France as a doctor, married al-Warraq's granddaughter, took up residence in a house in al-Sayyida, and brought Abd al-Azim into the world. Aziz Effendi educated his two sons, Amr and Surur, then Amr was appointed to the ministry of education and Surur to the railways. Rashwana married Sadiq Barakat, the flour merchant in al-Khurnfush. She was wedded to him in his house in Bayn al-Qasrayn. Amr married Shaykh Mu'awiya's oldest daughter, Radia, and Surur married Zaynab al-Naggar. The brothers moved into two adjacent houses on Bayt al-Qadi Square. When the Urabi Revolution came, Aziz supported it with all his heart, but Shaykh Mu'awiya supported it with his heart and his tongue and was incarcerated when the revolution was quashed.

Amr and Radia's marriage took place in the period following the shaykh's release, but the shaykh was not permitted to attend the wedding ceremony for he died a week after the engagement was announced and the opening sura read. Aziz Effendi was blessed with good health, longevity, and a happy marriage and did not suffer poverty or deprivation. He enjoyed close family ties with his relatives on Khayrat Square and in al-Sayyida and Suq al-Zalat. His children venerated him just as he rejoiced in their education, entry into government service, and sporting of suits and tarbooshes. As the days passed, he began to take pride in his younger brother's status and rank, especially once he was confident of his faith, observance of religious duties, and loyalty; that their two families could sit together around the table whenever he visited; and that they could walk together around al-Hussein and al-Qarafa. God was kind to him. He witnessed the birth of his grandchildren and was afforded a chaste departure at the end, for he died kneeling on his prayer mat one morning in autumn at home in al-Ghuriya. He was buried next to his father in the family enclosure, which later became known as "The Enclosure of Nagm al-Din."

Iffat Abd al-Azim Pasha

She was born and grew up in the family villa on Sarayat Road in East Abbasiya. She was the last of Abd al-Azim Pasha Dawud and Farida Husam's offspring after Lutfi, Ghassan, Halim, and Fahima. Iffat was born for great beauty. Blending her Syrian mother's fairness and father's tanned complexion, her cheeks were rosy and wheat-colored while a look of dominion and cunning could be detected in her black almond eyes. She lived comfortably in the elegant villa surrounded by rank and medals, and so, like other members of her family, got up onto feet rooted firmly in pride, superiority, and conceit. From the start, her father did not want his daughters to be illiterate, or near illiterate, like the girls in other branches of the family. Nor did he view their education as a preliminary to a career, which was how he saw it for the daughters of the poor among the general public. He therefore elected to give them a sophisticated education that he believed would set them up to marry eminent men. He found what he was looking for in the European schools, more particularly La Mère de Dieu. Iffat studied French, English, belles lettres, home economics, and music. Her soul was imbued with foreign tradition so that in taste, mentality, and heritage she appeared European to the observer. Although she never uttered a word to dishonor Islam, she knew nothing of her religion or history, and although she lived through the 1919 Revolution, she displayed no affiliation to her country other than some superficial enthusiasm for her father's political position born out of pride and family sentiment.

Yet her natural impulses revolted against all this, for from childhood her heart inclined to Amer, a relative on her father's side. In those days family ties meant more than class, status, rank, and fortune. Visits to Bayt al-Qadi, with their unusual scenes, peasant food, and Radia's mysteries, were enjoyable excursions for the Dawud family, though their sense of superiority never left them. Amer and Iffat's mutual affection thus met no opposition, indeed was welcomed, in Abd al-Azim's house. Expectations for daughters were, in any case, different to expectations for sons: the Dawud family could give a daughter to an acceptable son from Amr's family, but if a son coveted one of Amr or Surur's daughters, it constituted a serious aberration and had to be firmly suppressed. Amr's gentle manners allowed him to tolerate such a position and he looked for reasons to excuse it. It did not, however, escape the vicious tongue of Surur, who was consequently not as close to hearts in al-Murakibi or Dawud's families. When the need arose he would comment ironically, "How come the great family of Ata has forgotten the pantofles and the shop in al-Salihiya? How come Dawud's family has forgotten Uncle Yazid and Farga al-Sayyad?"

When the time came for Iffat to marry, the pasha had a beautiful house in Bayn al-Ganayin built, where she turned to meet the happy married life that would shatter the theories of its opponents. True, from the beginning she behaved like a princess whom circumstances had placed amid the herd, and the new setup created certain tensions between her and Amer's sisters, Surur's daughters, Shakira when she became her sister-in-law, and even Radia herself despite her friendship with Farida Husam. But the quarrels never reached the point of rupture or enmity; traditional bonds of friendship always triumphed. As for the married couple, they lived in sweetness and peace. Amer submitted fully to his beloved's strong will; he seldom raised an angry voice and they never argued. Iffat gave birth to Shakir, Qadri, and Fayyid but she was not able to extend the umbrella of her authority over them. Shakir hurt her pride and Qadri aroused her fear and anxiety. Yet the three were good examples of nobility and success. The July Revolution came, then successive defeats, then victory and peace, then clouds of strife and crime gathered once more. Meanwhile, Iffat sought refuge in the fort of the observer and let none of this worry her except insofar as her family and children were directly affected. She grew old and her arrogant tendencies calmed. Despite the stream of events, she lived happily with the love of her life, children, and grandchildren until Amer disappeared from her world in a blink of an eye, in the middle of a conversation. Thereafter, her life was silent and overshadowed with constant gloom.

Ata al-Murakibi

He started out as a boy in the shop of the Moroccan Gal'ad al-Mughawiri in al-Salihiya. The man scooped him up as an orphan, raised him, and gave him lodgings in the shop. The boy proved himself capable and trustworthy and stayed with his master until he was an able-bodied adolescent of medium height with burly features and a large head. Gal'ad married him to his only daughter, Sakina, and made him his deputy in the shop. He moved in with him at the house in al-Ghuriya, as neighbors of Yazid and his son, Aziz. When Gal'ad and his wife died, Sakina became the legal owner of the shop but in effect it passed to Ata. He wore the gentle manners of a merchant over his coarse features so was able to make friends with Yazid and

Shaykh al-Qalyubi. Sakina was moderately pretty but her body was worn down with frailty and she did not conceive for some time. Then, after a difficult delivery that nearly cost her life, she gave birth to Ni'ma. Ni'ma inherited her mother's wide black eyes, soft brown skin, and abundant chestnut hair, and she was healthy too. Sakina was a good neighbor and won Farga al-Sayyad's affection, paving the way for Ni'ma's marriage to Aziz at the appropriate time.

Each night, Shaykh al-Qalyubi, Yazid, and Ata would meet at the Shurbini Coffee Shop in Darb al-Ahmar. The men watched Napoleon Bonaparte lead his troops past the shrine of al-Hussein on his horse and lived through his campaign's vicissitudes, including the two Cairo uprisings. Yazid was nearly killed in the second. They witnessed Muhammad Ali's rule, the Mamluk massacre, and the upheaval the leader brought the country and its people. Though Shaykh al-Qalyubi was distinguished by his religious education, his tight bond to his people and heritage meant he was close to his two companions sentimentally. He was conscious of their greed and ignorance but ignored people's deficiencies and satisfied himself with their amicable side and friendship. He invited them to his house in Suq al-Zalat on several occasions, though only once was he invited back to the house in al-Ghuriya. He preferred Yazid to Ata, for he saw in the former the fundamentals of chivalry, integrity, and piety, which the other lacked. Nevertheless, he never tired of Ata or considered spurning him. Ata carried on content and amiable until his wife, Sakina, died, a year after their daughter Ni'ma married Yazid's son Aziz. He then surprised the whole quarter by marrying the rich widow, Huda al-Alawzi. She lived in the old house opposite the pantofle shop; did this tale then have the usual preface with no one noticing?

"Things will change," al-Qalyubi said to Yazid. "Huda Hanem will not be happy for her husband to remain in the shop."

Ata began to think with the head of a manager who had not

yet had the opportunity to use his talents. He consulted rich influential neighbors and skilled Jews about his affairs and promptly purchased land and began building the great mansion on Khayrat Square. As time passed, he bought a farm in Beni Suef too and had a country mansion built there. Huda Hanem al-Alawzi gave birth to Mahmud and Ahmad. Ata started studying farming and cementing relations with his new neighbors. Wealth unveiled his hidden talents and strength of character, as it did his greed, miserliness, and endless hunger for money. Contrary to expectations, he imposed total authority on his wife and those he dealt with, until Shaykh al-Qalyubi compared him to the leader who came to Egypt as a simple soldier and turned into a giant at the vortex of a vast empire, though the emperor of Beni Suef was not half as bad as Napoleon.

His relations with his old friends weakened but he never stopped visiting Ni'ma and Aziz in al-Ghuriya. He would descend on the quarter in his carriage, ignoring looks of envy and proffering occasional gifts on festival days. He would invite the family to the mansion on Khayrat Square, so Rashwana, Amr, and Surur became good friends with Mahmud and Ahmad. However, there were always limits to his expressions of generosity and his two sons were probably more sympathetic to their poor sister, Ni'ma, than Ata was himself. He naturally sent his sons to school but, like their cousins Amr and Surur, they ran out of breath with the primary school certificate. This did not especially bother Ata and he began preparing them to farm beside him. He was delighted by Mahmud's keen response and steel character, but Ahmad dashed his hopes and in the end he left him in despair at his docile ways. Bakri al-Arshi, the head of the Mamluk family on the next-door farm, had two daughters, Nazli and Fawziya, equal in beauty and sophistication. Ata requested they marry his sons, Mahmud and Ahmad, and the marriages were celebrated in a joint wedding feast brought to life by Abduh al-Hamuli and Almuz.

Ata lived through the Urabi Revolution. His emotions were not conquered via nationalism but by way of land and money. So when the waves of the revolution rose high and he was sure of its victory, he announced support and donated money, hiding the pain this caused him, and when hostile forces assailed it and its failure glimmered on the horizon he declared allegiance to the khedive. When the British Occupation began he was gripped once more by anxiety over events whose effect on his land he did not know, but his father-in-law, Bakri al-Arshi, assured him, "The English won't leave the country and we won't leave the British Empire in our lifetime."

When he felt he was approaching the end he said to his son Mahmud, "Here's some advice that is more valuable than money. Consider the farm your country and devote all your heart to it. Beware of sermons and slogans."

Ata died of old age and his wife joined him a month later. Mahmud and Ahmad inherited the entire fortune and Aziz and Ni'ma's hope was forever extinguished.

Aql Hamada al-Qinawi

Khan Ga'far was where he was born and Bayt al-Qadi, Bayn al-Qasrayn, Watawit, Ibn Khaldun, East Abbasiya, Bayn al-Ganayin, and Khayrat Square were where he played, wandered, made friends, and loved. He was the second child of Sadriya and Hamada al-Qinawi, borrowing his beautiful eyes from his mother and his flat nose and sturdy body from his father, though he was not very tall. His father loved him dearly and hallowed him with great glory as the heir apparent. The man watched happily and proudly as his son achieved in school and abundantly compensated for his own ignorance and illiteracy. From childhood, Aql was interested in religion and engineering. He enrolled in the faculty of engineering but continued his religious readings and was also drawn to Islamic philosophy. He was swept away in a current of conflicting ideas and remained in a state of confusion all his life.

As he roved about the branches of the family he was attracted to his aunt Samira's daughter Hanuma. He wanted her reserved for him but the girl said to her mother, "He is obviously shorter than me. He isn't suitable!" He was shocked and his limbs blazed with anger. Despite his doubts, he continued to pray and fast assiduously; he could not be confident but refused not to believe and sought refuge in his religious duties. Doubt suffused his very being and he could not connect with anything. He watched the decline of the Wafd, detested the abstruseness of the Marxists, and held the duplicitous Misr al-Fatah in contempt. He eschewed the July Revolution, though the sentiment had nothing to do with the opposition of the landowning class, the class to which he ultimately belonged. He was very sad about his sister, Warda, and father. When he graduated he found a job in an engineering office and began thinking seriously about marriage. Perhaps it would deliver him from the emptiness that suffocated him. He liked Hikmat, his brother-in-law's sister, so proposed to her and married her. They moved into an apartment in a small building near his uncle Amer's house in Bayn al-Ganayin. He desperately wanted children, as did his father's relatives, but it became apparent he was sterile. He was deeply saddened and pained. "Don't trust doctors and don't despair of God's mercy," said his grandmother Radia.

Life stood before him in the image of unattainable desires: always sweet and insurmountable. When there was no one left in the family house and Sadriya was all on her own, he said to her, "You know I'm devoted to you. Come and live with us in Bayn al-Ganayin."

But his mother replied smiling, "I won't leave al-Hussein or your grandmother."

He strove harder to perform his religious duties and reap the fruit of his talents as an engineer. One day he said to his wife,

Hikmat, "I don't want you to spend a day with me that you don't want to."

She frowned for a minute then said, "I am completely happy, praise God."

Doubts about the future of his relationship with his wife began to assail him. He was also possessed by concerns about the future of his country, which was moving from one crisis to the next. He did not breathe easily again until Sadat's time. He found in the infitah policy a great commercial opportunity that made him forget his doubts and misgivings. He chose property as his business arena, using his savings and the sale of his portion of his father's property. He made an immense amount of money and worked with remarkable energy until he was over sixty. At that point he asked himself, "Now what?"

He thought for a long time then said to Hikmat, "I'm bored of working. It's time we enjoyed our money."

"What do you lack?" she asked guilelessly.

He laughed sarcastically. "Travel. We must travel," he said. "We'll see the world and taste its delights."

She was bewildered. She knew nothing of the world beyond her father's village and Bayn al-Ganayin, nor did she have any desire to. When he saw her confusion he said, "With me you won't need a translator."

He said to himself: If she hates the idea I'll go alone. But as usual she obeyed him. She began packing suitcases. A spark of doubt shot out from his belly and he examined his surroundings for a while. The airplane will probably burst into flames. I know how these things work! he said to himself. But the airplane did not burst into flames. Nor did his misgivings abate.

Amr Aziz Yazid al-Misri

He was born and grew up in the house in al-Ghuriya with Rashwana and Surur. He took the essence of the quarter into his heart, lovingly and eagerly, thus Egyptian peasant traditions swaggered in his soul and his sleeves exuded their spirit and religion. He was probably the dearest of the three to Aziz and Ni'ma, as he resembled his father in his well-proportioned body, wheat-colored skin, and wide clear eyes. He was the sensible one, steering and checking Surur and Rashwana as they played and wandered between Bab al-Mutawalli and the fountain of Bayn al-Qasrayn. Later he became known for his wisdom and was consulted on all kinds of matters. He enjoyed a similar status among his uncles, Mahmud and Ahmad, and his cousin Abd al-Azim. He faithfully performed his religious duties from childhood and played the role of policeman in Surur's frequent outbursts. He entered Qur'an school, memorized what he could from the Holy Qur'an, and learned the principles of reading and writing. At the age of twelve he started primary school and, after much strain and effort, obtained the primary school certificate. With Dawud Pasha's help he was appointed a bookkeeper in the ministry of education.

He always earned the respect of his superiors and colleagues. He enriched his life with friendships, enlightened it reading the Qur'an and writings of the saints, and varied his sphere of activity through generosity that exuded love of religion and the world. Thus, he attended Sufi gatherings in al-Sanadiqiya, listened to al-Hamuli at weddings, and met his good friends at the Misri Club. He was peaceful by nature, achieving through clemency what could not be achieved through force or anger. The moment his father pronounced marriage a good idea he gave it the welcome of a robust and pious young man. The choice fell on Radia, the eldest daughter of his father's friend Shaykh Mu'awiya. She was wedded to him in a newly built house on Bayt al-Qadi Square. It was the beginning of a successful and prosperous marriage. Radia was his opposite. She was nervous and stubborn and her mysteries were unrestrained; were it not for his peaceful nature and clemency, things would not have proceeded along the same peaceful course with his dignity at home remaining intact. He did not escape Radia's influence, however, for he believed in her heritage and popular medicine and was obliged to let her visit saints' tombs, even if he would have preferred her to stay in the house like his brother's wife, Zaynab, and the hanem wives of Mahmud, Ahmad, and Abd al-Azim. "They are all nice hanems but they are ignorant and have no hand in matters of the Unknown," Radia told him haughtily.

At the same time, she made his house an abode of mercy and love and gave birth to Sadriya, Amer, Matariya, Samira, Habiba, Hamid, and Qasim. Unlike Surur, Amr took pride in his relatives: the mansion on Khayrat Square, the villa on Sarayat Road, the land, money, and rank; and his house enjoyed everyone's affection accordingly. Carriage after carriage came by, transporting to him the nobles and hanems of Beni Suef and the family of Dawud Pasha with its hanems. They would sit around Amr's table, shower him with gifts, take pleasure in Radia's quirks and heritage, and commend the bravery of her father, the hero of the Urabi Revolution. It was these profound friendships that opened the door of marriage into the families of Ata and Dawud, elevating and strengthening Amr's status and provoking dissension between him and Surur, which could have ruined their relationship, were it not for solid foundations and long memories. Surur often commented regretfully, "If Huda al-Alawzi had died before Ata al-Murakibi we would have inherited!"

"God's will is unopposed," Amr would reply.

He surmounted any such twinges with his tolerant faith and it was his habit, when feeling resentful, to remind himself of the many blessings granted him, like good health and children. True, the day Dawud's family smothered Lutfi's affection for Matariya he erupted in anger and let Radia rant, saying to himself: They aren't wrong when they say relatives are scorpions!

But it was a cloud that quickly dissolved under the beams of an eternal sun.

His heart was also full of patriotism. He was too young to share his father's disappointment at the demise of the Urabi Revolution, but he often watched the occupying troops circling the old quarter like tourists and his heart was soon brimming with the speeches of Mustafa Kamil and Muhammad Farid. His excitement reached a climax with the 1919 Revolution; he adored its leader and joined in the civil servants' strike. He remained loyal to the leader even when his important relatives, Mahmud, Ahmad, and Abd al-Azim, broke away, and eagerly followed the leader's successor, Mustafa al-Nahhas, by dishing out cups of sherbet the day the treaty was signed. Amr whole-heartedly supported the leader against the new king and, despite the weak heart that was soon to kill him, was angry when he was discharged from government service.

He bore his children's burdens while they were in his care and shared in their worries once they had each settled in their own homes. "We always dream of rest but there's no rest in life," he would say. He sought refuge in his faith and left mankind to the Creator. How many hopes he had pinned on Qasim and to what effect? When he was pensioned off a melancholy spread over him. Heart disease descended out of nowhere, curbing his movements and pleasures and plunging him into the depths of depression. One evening, sitting in the Misri Club, he fell unconscious. He was carried to his bed dying and passed away in Radia's arms a little before dawn.

Ghayn

Ghassan Abd al-Azim Dawud

HE WAS BORN AND GREW UP IN THE VILLA on Sarayat Road, the second child of Abd al-Azim Pasha Dawud. He was perhaps the only one of Abd al-Azim Pasha's sons not to inherit any of his mother, Farida Hanem's, good looks. He was small and thin with a dark complexion and most of the time his face wore a frown and conveyed a look of disgust, as though someone was squeezing a lemon in his mouth. It was as if he was born to detest the world and everything in it. He would shut himself off in his room at the villa, take walks through the quiet streets to the east in the shade of their tall trees, and venture deep into the open desert. He did not make friends with any of the neighbors and he did not form a fraternal bond with either of his brothers, Lutfi and Halim, or his sisters, Fahima and Iffat. On the rare occasions he played with his brother Halim in the garden of the villa or in the street, it ended in misunderstanding and argument. Once it concluded in a fight in which Ghassan was defeated despite being the elder. His father took him to visit relatives, Amr's family in particular, and he was once invited with his family to the Ata family mansion on Khayrat Square. He would look on but barely utter a word and did not make a single friend; they called him "Men's Enemy" and mocked his silent, nauseated countenance, thin body, eternal reticence, and reclusive haughtiness. Gleams of hunger may have shone in his eyes as he gazed at his beautiful female cousins but they were not accompanied by a smile or gesture.

"You must stop secluding yourself," his father would tell him.

"I know where to find peace and quiet and I'm not interested in anything else," he would cut back.

"What do you do locked in your room?"

"Listen to records and read."

But he did not reveal any literary or intellectual talents.

He adopted his father's political views, probably because they fitted his sense of superiority and inborn contempt for the masses. He saw nationalist pursuits and popular leadership as a variety of banal political posturing. It did not escape his attention that he was held in lower esteem than other members of his family, and the degree of ignorance that prevented him from attaining the eminence his social status and class arrogance merited challenged his self-importance. He was hard on himself and put himself through intolerable and unsustainable exertions, staying up all night studying only to gain average marks that were just good enough to take him from one grade to the next at the tail end of the top students. He put himself through torture in order to excel but to no avail. He eyed the victorious with resentment and respect and was filled with distress at his own incompetence. How could he be incompetent when his grandfather, father, and older brother were all pashas? The future loomed before him as a stark battle bristling with provocation and aggravation. Nor could he find consolation in religion since, like his brothers and sisters, he knew it only in name, not in substance. Thus, he worshiped work and gave himself to it wholly, only to be forced to content himself at the end with the tiny fruit his arid land could produce.

When he enrolled in the faculty of law, he found his cousin Labib, Surur Effendi's son, crowned in a halo of admiration for his achievements and tender age, which compounded Ghassan's depression and wretchedness. He took exception to the divine decree that conferred genius on his penniless cousin, a pauper's son, while denying it to him, a descendant of pashas and high-ranking lawyers and doctors. Perhaps part of his contempt for nationalism was to do with the fervor of his poor relations, Amr and Surur's families. He was unenthusiastic about the 1919 Revolution as it unfolded and quickly sought refuge with his father and his family on the side of those opposing it. When he graduated, he watched his cousin be appointed to the public prosecutor's office while he was left behind despite his noble descent and late nights. With the help of his father, the grand councilor, he was assigned to the legal department at the ministry of education, and started his career angry and peeved though he had no right to be. He became known in the workplace for introversion, industry, and ignorance; all his promotions were through the intercession of his father. He continued to seclude himself both at the office and at the villa. He had no friends or girlfriends and only left the library, which he built up year after year, when absolutely necessary. He could sometimes be seen alone in a public garden or at the club, or sneaking with extreme caution into a secret high-class brothel.

"It's time you thought about marriage," said Farida Hanem Husam.

He looked at her with surprise and annoyance and muttered, "This is all there is."

He had several reasons to hate the thought of marriage. For a start, it would invade his sacred solitude, which he could not abandon, and he was afraid the right girl would reject his job or family due to the various shortcomings of which he was not unaware. Farida worried about him constantly, especially after Abd al-Azim Pasha's death, when she sensed her time was approaching and that she would be leaving him in a big empty villa. The July Revolution brought afflictions he had not predicted. "Have we sunk so low as to be ruled by a band of illiterate army fellows?" he asked himself anxiously. He watched what happened to his family's rank and the value of its lawyers and doctors in dismay, asking himself, "Should I now be sorry the Wafd rabble have gone?"

"I'll be joining your father sometime soon. You need a wife and children," Farida said to him.

"Bachelorhood is the final solace," he replied rudely.

He persisted in this malevolent obstinacy and his resolve was not shaken after his mother's death. He retired at the beginning of the 1970s and went on living alone like a ghost. It was as though the world could offer him nothing but enduring health, and his only pleasure was to be found in food and books, then television and the new maid.

Faruq Hussein Qabil

THE FOURTH CHILD OF SAMIRA and Hussein Qabil, he was born and grew up on Ibn Khaldun Street. Like his brothers and sisters, he greeted the world with a slender, vigorous body and good looks and he had a promising, brilliant mind. He was, however, brought up in the disciplined climate that prevailed on the family after Hussein Qabil's death. From childhood, he dreamed of becoming a doctor and, with strong determination, fulfilled his dream, surmounting the obstacles of the system. His heart was divided between enthusiasm for the July Revolution, because of his birth and a disposition he shared with his brother Hakim, and occasional aversion to it out of sympathy for the Muslim Brothers and affection for his brother Salim, who had been thrown in prison. He found deliverance from the contradictions by concerning himself with his work. When he got his license to practice he opened a private clinic alongside his hospital work. He fell in love with a colleague, Doctor Aqila Thabit, and they married and moved into a modern apartment in New Cairo. Faruq was greatly saddened by the fate of his brother Hakim and the absence of his other brother, Salim. Samira's sons learned the strength of their tenacity just as, like their mother, they learned to stand firm in the face of adversity. He was careful not to let his political views be known outside the family environment, taking the suffering of his brothers as a lesson, and devoted himself to his work. In this arena he achieved a unique position as a surgeon, and his wife, similarly, held high-ranking posts as a midwife. She gave birth to two daughters, who gravitated competently to medicine. Faruq was among the few who believed in Sadat's politics, with the exception of his unregulated infitah policy, whose gates opened with an exuberance that brought the country significant economic problems. Thus, he did not belong to the section of the population that rejoiced at Sadat's death. He once commented to his uncle Amr, "Sadat took Gamal Abdel Nasser's place and so was assassinated in his place."

He was remembered as a rare doctor, meaning that he always stood by his principles and never overcharged for his troubles.

Fayyid Amer Amr

The third son of Amer and Iffat, like his two brothers he was born and grew up in the house in Bayn al-Ganayin. With his fair complexion, beautiful eyes, and slender figure he bore a close resemblance to his grandmother, Farida Husam. He soaked up a good portion of the heritage of Amr and Radia and the old quarter but was sated by the customs of his other grandparents, Farida and Abd al-Azim Pasha Dawud. From childhood, he adored the law and the glory of legal office, just as he adored modern culture—cinema and radio, then television. He loved his two grandfathers, Amr and Abd al-Azim, but took no interest in the Wafd, nor indeed any other political party. He graduated from law school among the top students and, with his achievements and Abd al-Azim Pasha's standing, was immediately appointed to the public prosecutor's office. Of Amer and Iffat's children, he was perhaps the only one whose behavior and ideas did not cause them worry, in contrast to his brothers, Shakir and Qadri. When he announced one day that he was in love with a student from law school, a girl called Magida al-Arshi, Iffat became agitated because of bitter past experience. However, she was happy when she was reassured that the girl was a doctor's daughter, a doctor's granddaughter, and from a very good, suitable family. "It's the first wedding to whet the appetite!" she remarked to Amer.

Fayyid married and moved into an apartment in New Cairo. He was not averse to the July Revolution, although it invalidated his grandfather and uncle's rank. Indeed, he was rather drawn to it and made no attempt to hide this from his mother and father.

"It came at the perfect time," he said.

Fayyid advanced with familiar speed until he became a councilor. His attitude to the revolution and its leader remained the same; even the ordeal of June 5 did not change his mind, though it rent his heart. As for Sadat, he supported him in his war and turning of a new page in democracy but had severe misgivings about the peace plan, then cursed him for the infitah policy and relapse of democracy. Thus, while he did not condone his assassination, he was not sad and believed Sadat had got what he deserved. Fayyid only had one daughter, who specialized in chemistry. Iffat named her Farida after her mother.

Farga al-Sayyad

She appeared in al-Ghuriya at the age of fourteen with a strong body and nice face, walking about in a blue gallabiya, carrying a basket with fish and a set of scales on her head. She was forced to foray from her house in al-Sukariya after her father died and her mother was paralyzed, and was looked after by neighborhood customs and piety. One day a robust man with an accent from outside Cairo called her over to buy some fish. She lowered her basket to the ground and, squatting behind it, began balancing the weights. He gazed at her for a while and said, "Dear girl, you're so sweet."

"Do you want fish or the scales smashed in your face?" she replied rudely.

The man snorted unconsciously. She got to her feet, appealing to the onlookers. Some men dived on the stranger and the situation became aggravated. However, a man they recognized—Ata al-Murakibi—stepped forward from the crowd and shouted, "Praise the Prophet." He laughed and said, "He's an Alexandrian. He lives in my building. He's not familiar with local custom. When they snort it's like when we take a deep breath." Ata recovered his neighbor and took him to his shop.

For his part, Ata saw the man's arrival as a bad omen since it dragged in its wake an army of infidels, Napoleon's troops. "What brought you here?" he asked.

"The plague killed my family so I decided to leave Alexandria," he replied.

Things changed when Ata married his master's daughter, Sakina; he began to regard the Alexandrian's arrival as a good omen and started liking him. "Dear old Yazid, you brought blessings!"

Yazid al-Misri did not forget Farga al-Sayyad. He said to his friend, "I want to marry the fish seller." Ata al-Murakibi asked the mother for her daughter's hand and Farga was wedded to Yazid at his apartment in the house in al-Ghuriya. Ata al-Murakibi claimed that as soon as he closed the door on the bride and groom, the guests outside in the salon could hear the snorts boring a hole through the door, like water gurgling in a narghile. Yazid al-Misri was happy in his marriage and Farga gave birth to many children, of whom only Aziz and Dawud survived. The couple lived to see their grandchildren. One night, Yazid dreamed he saw a man who said he was Nagm al-Din, at whose tomb he sometimes prayed. He advised him, "Build your grave next to mine so we may come together as friends." Yazid did not waver. He constructed the enclosure in which he was buried and which, to this day, welcomes his deceased descendants from all over Cairo.

Fahima Abd al-Azim Pasha

She was known as The Flowers' Friend because of the long hours she spent in the garden of the villa on Sarayat Road. She was the most beautiful of Abd al-Azim's children and prettier than Farida Hanem Husam. She may not have been as clever as Iffat, but her heart was kinder and her soul purer. She was educated with her sister at La Mère de Dieu with the same end in mind, namely to prepare her to marry into high rank. Yet her marriage nonetheless came about in the traditional way, as she was engaged—by way of a neighbor—to a public prosecutor called Ali Tal'at. Abd al-Azim Pasha Dawud had a house built for her in Bayn al-Ganayin, as he had done for Iffat, and she was wedded to her groom there. The marriage was very successful and she gave birth to Dawud, Abd al-Azim, and Farida. However, the bad luck waiting round the corner for the family became proverbial. Fahima lost her children once they had made it through youth and raised hope: Dawud died of typhoid in his third year of law school, Abd al-Azim died of cholera a month after graduating from the faculty of science, and Farida died of rheumatism of the heart in secondary school. Profound grief distracted the parents to the point of renouncing the world. Ali Tal'at, then a councilor at the court of appeals in Cairo, requested his pension and devoted himself to worship and religious readings in constant seclusion at home or in the cemetery. Fahima, in contrast, who came from a family where religion crouched on the margins, began asking questions about fate and the day she would be united with her dead children once more. She started buying all the books she could find at the market about spirits, how to summon them, and secret powers, and finally put faith in Radia and the heritage she had previously looked on with a mocking smile.

"Have patience, dear daughter," her father, Abd al-Azim Pasha, said. "If only I could ransom myself for your children."

"You're goodness and blessings, Papa. May God prolong your life," she replied.

Each time he led the funeral procession of one of her young children, heading the cortege due to his advanced years, he felt anguished and somehow culpable. He found the eyes gazing at him in reverent silence oppressive. Ali Tal'at soon entered God's mercy, struck down by a severe flu, and Fahima found herself on her own in her kingdom of spirits. She lived long after the death of her parents and relatives from the respectable generation, which hallowed tradition and family ties, and became oblivious to everything except the telephone conversations she had with her sister, Iffat.

Qaf

Qasim Amr Aziz

THE LAST CHILD OF AMR AND RADIA, he was born and grew up in the house on Bayt al-Qadi Square and was the only one of the children who never left home. From the beginning, he was thin and lively and bore no obvious resemblance to either parent. However, when he laughed he called to mind his father, and anyone who saw him when he was agitated was reminded of Radia. The roof and the square with its tall trees were his playground and he lived life to the full in the winter rain and Khamsin wind. He was not given the opportunity to get close to any of his brothers or sisters, as the moment he reached adolescence they departed for their marital homes. Instead, he made friends with his uncle Surur's and the neighbors' children and found recreation at the homes of his married brothers and sisters and the families of Ata and Dawud. He was his mother's most devoted listener and the most believing follower of her dreams and spiritual tours about the mosques and shrines. Whenever his imagination played up he found in her a receptive ear and believing heart. One night in Ramadan he told her that he had seen a window of radiant light open in the sky for a few moments on the "Night of Power" and that another night he beheld a procession of demons through the gap in the mashrabiya. When still a boy, he gazed with interest at the girls in the family, alert and hungry before his time, and would hover in particular around Dananir, Gamila, and Bahiga, as well as the neighbors' girls and young women; even their wives did not escape his wicked desires. Yet he was pious, prayed, and fasted from an early age.

He entered Qur'an school reluctantly and learned the basic principles with a reticent heart and rebellious mind. He could never distinguish between school and the district prison in Gamaliya where wretched faces loomed behind the window bars. At an after-dinner gathering, Amr questioned him, "Don't you want to be like your brothers?"

"No way!" he shouted back.

His father frowned and warned him, "Don't force me to become strict with you."

Qasim's image of his father was shaken by the man's failure to prevent his cousin Ahmad's death and he, Qasim, was left to cry in vain. He liked the pleasure afforded by Gamila's embrace, although his heart would be seized by pain when he came to pray. He was constantly torn between love and prayer and Bahiga and his mother's vigilant eyes. One day, Radia caught him and Gamila on the roof among the chickens, rabbits, and cats. The moment she appeared they broke free from their embrace. Gamila flew off like a dove, blood rushing to her cheeks in shame. Radia glowered and, pointing her emaciated hand up to the sky over the roof, said, "God sees everything from up there."

Gamila vanished from sight when a suitable man came forward and Qasim added a broken heart to the anguish of death. He began to see rabbits' heads peeking out from under overturned earthenware jars and it was not long before he found himself confronting illusions alongside irksome school lessons and a mysterious smile in Bahiga's beautiful eyes. He expected her to be like her sister, Gamila, but found a sweet heart combined with a strong will. What good could come from their wordless exchange? "You two are the same age. He isn't suitable," Bahiga's mother, Sitt Zaynab, said to her.

And Radia told him, "It's important you focus your energy on school."

Amr spread his palms and pleaded, "Lord, be kind to me with this boy."

Qasim wept over the harsh ban. Sitting with his parents one evening, his father asked him why he was crying. "I'm thinking about Ahmad!"

Amr frowned. "That's ancient history. Even his own mother has forgotten him!" he exclaimed.

He began to gaze at things sadly and weep. When they were alone, Radia said to her husband, "The evil eye has taken our son."

"People envy his misfortune!" Amr replied angrily.

She perfumed him with incense, but when he inhaled its mysterious aroma he fell unconscious. His father took him to the doctor, who concluded it was a mild bout of epilepsy and there was nothing to fear; he needed rest and a change of atmosphere. They recalled the tragedy of Samira's daughter, Badriya. Once when his parents were present he gazed into space and said, "I will do anything you wish. . . ."

"Is this the illness rambling?" Amr asked.

"No. He is communicating with people in the Unknown," Radia replied confidently.

People learned of his condition and flocked to Bayt al-Qadi to try and revive him. They stared at him full of curiosity and apprehension. At Ata's mansion there was whispering.

"It's the root of madness that has long run through Radia's family," Shakira said to her mother.

At her house Sitt Zaynab said the same to Surur, while Radia asserted her knowledge of such things to Amr and told him with faith and conviction, "Don't be afraid or sad. Trust in God."

She took her son around the shrines and burned incense in every corner of the house. Qasim renounced school in contempt and began roaming the alleys and wandering about the houses of his brothers and sisters and relatives on Khayrat Square, Sarayat Road, and Bayn al-Ganayin. Everywhere he went he would be given something to drink and would make some enigmatic remarks about the future as he saw it. Events fulfilled his prophecies and he became known as "The Shaykh." People no longer dared to make fun of him.

"It's God's will," Mahmud Bey said to a dejected Amr. "You're a believer. The boy has a secret that no one but God knows. He reads my thoughts. I have to think carefully before I do anything."

"But what about the future? How will he make a living?" Amr asked.

His aunt Shahira was present and said, "God does not forget any of his creation so why should He forget one of his saints?"

Qasim's reputation was spread as a legend. Troubled rich men began arriving with gifts, then money, and the family was forced to set aside a room on the first floor to receive his visitors. Amr was amazed as his son's fortune grew and overtook that of all his brothers together. His worries faded with time until it seemed Qasim was made for this role. Qasim exchanged his European clothes for a gallabiya, cloak, and turban, let his beard grow, and divided his time between receiving visitors and praying on the roof. Even his mother—the mistress of ancient knowledge—became one of his students and disciples. He opened his heart to the sorrows of his family and plunged into their dramas. He paid the last honors for their dead and blessed them in the cavity of their tombs. One day, when he was in his thirties, his heart began to beat in a way that brought rose-scented memories of the past flooding back. A tender voice called him to leave the house. He wrapped his cloak around him, went out, and headed straight to his uncle's house next door. Bahiga met him with amazement, asking herself what had prompted him to burst into her desperate solitude now. They gazed at one another as they had in the carefree old days.

"I dreamed you were beckoning me," he said.

She smiled weakly.

"A voice from the Unknown told me the time has come for us to marry," he continued. He promptly stood up and left. He returned home and told his mother, "I want to marry. Propose to Bahiga on my behalf."

Radia told herself that the saints had all married and produced children. When Labib came to visit she told him the news. Labib consulted his cousins Amer and Hamid, and they all agreed Qasim was capable of bearing the burden of a family; the matter rested with Bahiga. Amazingly, Bahiga consented. Some said it was desperation, others said it was the old love. Either way, she was married to him as soon as the old house had been rejuvenated with new furniture. The wedding took place in near silence because of the gloom that reigned during the war; it was celebrated with antiaircraft fire. Years went by without children. Then, one day, Bahiga gave birth to her only son, al-Naqshabandi. He was handsome, like his uncle Labib, and extremely healthy and intelligent. He graduated as an engineer the year of the Setback and, shortly before the 1970s, was sent on a delegation to West Germany. The situation in his country was a burden on his personal well-being so he decided to emigrate. He took an important post at a steel manufacturer after obtaining his doctorate, married a German girl, and settled in Germany for good. Bahiga was deeply saddened while Qasim, who was never sad, bade him farewell with his heart but did not shed a tear.

Qadri Amer Amr

He was born and grew up in the house in Bayn al-Ganayin, the middle son of Amer and Iffat. From childhood he shone in play, industry, and imagination. From childhood too, he was kindled by reading and interested in public life and, unlike his two brothers, was to find he sided with the Marxists. He was passionate about art and literature, despite a gift for science, and laid the foundations for his private library when still in the first year of secondary school. He was a near image of his father, though taller and more robust, and naturally rash, which got him into difficulty. How great was Amer's surprise when his son was arrested amid a group of Marxists. The man rushed to his father-in-law, Abd al-Azim Pasha, who took steps to have Qadri released on the pretext of youth. The pasha was nevertheless alarmed. "How did such a boy emerge from your house?" he asked Amer and Iffat.

"We haven't been lax in raising them, but others have sneaked into their lives and corrupted them," Amer replied timidly.

Qadri entered the faculty of engineering with his name on the security forces' blacklist. Halim warned his sister the situation could jeopardize his future, and Hamid did the same with his brother Amer. Qadri was repeatedly arrested and released while an engineering student. He was at one time drawn to Shazli, his aunt Matariya's son, because of their shared culture. But he found Shazli agnostic, the antithesis of his own rational Sufism, so he lost patience and moved on. When he graduated as an engineer he shunned the civil service and worked in the engineering office of a retired teacher of his. He was a competent engineer but his reputation was marred by his politics. His mother was keen that he marry—to sort him out, on the one hand, and to compensate her loss in the case of Shakir, on the other. For his part, he welcomed the idea. She wanted one of his uncle Lutfi Pasha's daughters for him but did not find the enthusiasm she had hoped for and guessed it was because of his bad reputation. Her anxiety was compounded when neighbors rejected him because they doubted his piety and, consequently, the validity of the marriage. Qadri grew angry with the idea of marriage, just as he was with the bourgeoisie in general. He began to believe his uncles Ghassan and Halim were wise to forsake it.

By the July Revolution his political activism had ceased, but his ideology and friends were the same and the cloud shrouding his reputation had not dissipated. He made palpable progress in his career and it looked set to continue, but then he was sent to prison for the third time. His father appealed to some important officers who had been former students of his. They indulged him and Qadri was released. When the revolution became linked with the Eastern Bloc he inclined toward it and began to see dimensions he had not seen before. Perhaps it was this that made the national catastrophe of June 5 easier for him to bear; he saw it as a clear beginning to securing Soviet influence in Egypt and a step closer to total revolution when the time was ripe. Perhaps this was what made him greet the victory of October 6 with an exasperation he could not conceal. He expended all his logic and learning in negating its meaning and portraying it as a charade. He said to himself: Victory for the bourgeoisie equals victory for reactionism! It was for this reason he opposed Sadat the moment his political strategy became clear and why he detested him both in life and in death, despite the wealth that unexpectedly came his way in the days of the infitah policy. He was one of the flood of men sentenced in September 1981. He was freed with the rest a few days before his father died to resume his successful job and frustrated hopes.

Lam

Labib Surur Aziz

HE WAS SURUR AND ZAYNAB'S FIRST CHILD. He had a radiant, handsome face, which resembled his mother's, and a slender body, below average in height, which seemed designed for a girl. Amazingly, he was calm and composed from childhood, as though he had been born fully mature. Playing for him consisted in standing outside the front door watching the world go by; or following the movements of his cousin Qasim, who was a few years older than him, as he got up to mischief like others his age; or walking around the square cracking almonds. Radia would call him over and say affectionately, "Sensible boy!"

She would also say of him, "The father is an idiot and the mother is a fool, so where did the brains come from?"

When he was just four years old, encouraged by his composure and avoidance of childish mischief, Surur Effendi sent him to Qur'an school. He thought it would not be a waste of time if he spent a year or two there without understanding or grasping anything. But in those two years he acquired enough knowledge to satisfy the shaykh. "Your nephew, Labib, is an amazing boy. You must start him at primary school," the shaykh said to Labib's uncle, Amr Effendi. In those days no one advanced to primary school below the age of eight or nine, so Labib's father presented him for the entrance exam without taking it seriously and his success came as a surprise. His studies began when he was only six and he progressed with success year after year, causing astonishment around the family. Even more astonishing was the way he applied himself to his homework without encouragement or incentives, or anyone's help, until he obtained the primary school certificate aged only ten. His age and talent enabled him to enter one of the king's special schools free of charge, and he progressed through secondary school with similar success. As a teenager, he resisted the temptations he encountered around family or in the street, obeying his mother's warnings and deliberately spurning whatever might impede his industry and uprightness. Thus, he obtained the baccalaureate at the age of sixteen. The teachers college was the preferred and appropriate option in the family's circumstances, but the ambitious young man announced he wanted to go to law school.

"It's the school for leaders!" muttered Surur, worried but hopeful.

"Let's get Abd al-Azim's advice," said Amr.

The pasha was impressed with the young man's history so took steps for him to enter law school, again with the fees waived. Labib's father had his first long-trouser suit made for him. He went off to law school to be gazed at with amazement; sarcastic comments about the "Elementary Law School" and "The King's Kindergarten" buzzed around him and attitudes did not change until he proved his ability and potential. He did not hesitate to join in the demonstrations and distribute pamphlets when the 1919 Revolution broke out, though his activities mostly took place in shelter and safety. He was conscious of the class differences between him and his colleagues and it left a residue in his soul. Yet he overcame it with his natural calm and inherent wisdom. It never worried him that he only had one suit, was not part of a social scene or life of luxury, and traveled in second class on the tram. He avoided troubling his father with requests that might challenge his resources; he was always, as Radia said, very sensible.

His patience and industry bore fruit. He obtained his law degree at the age of eighteen, placed in the top ten. He was obstructed from working for the public prosecutor's office not because of his roots—in deference to Abd al-Azim Dawud—but because it refused to appoint a minor as an assistant prosecutor! Thus, it was agreed he should take a clerical post until he reached majority, at which point he joined the public prosecutor's office. This enabled Aziz's family to hold its head high, gaining for them a foothold in the upper ranks of the bureaucracy next to Dawud and Ata's families, and prompting jealousy, resentment, and astonishment in every branch of the family, including those closest to him—namely his cousins. Surur Effendi walked tall as though *he* was the public prosecutor. His tongue grew more vicious and left a nasty mark in people's hearts and he became insufferable.

Yet contrary to expectation and logic, winds of anxiety would blow around Labib. He constantly proved competent and impartial as a prosecutor and judge, thus earning trust and respect, but his family's circumstances decreed that his marriage had to wait until he had assisted in his brothers' education and sisters' weddings. Meanwhile, impulses he had long restrained erupted, demanding compensation for what they had missed out on during childhood, youth, and adolescence. All of a sudden he craved wine and women. He began indulging in riotous behavior and moral depravity while observing the customs of his profession as far as possible. He grew accustomed to this lifestyle until it took him over completely. He did not consider changing even after he was discharged from his family obligations, despite the threat to his reputation and damage to his health.

The July Revolution shook the status of the law and its men. He was overcome with gloom as an old Wafdist on the one hand, and as a lawyer on the other. He continued visiting every branch of the family and began keenly following the revolution's effect on them, careful not to give himself away. His cousin Hamid was probably the closest to him. Labib once whispered to his cousin, "What's the ruse? We have before us a man claiming leadership with a revolver in his hand!"

When he was head of the court of appeals in Alexandria and approaching retirement, he had a sudden upturn and burst with all his energies down the path of prayer and matrimony. He prayed to the point of becoming a dervish and for the first time considered marrying his cousin Dananir. He had not forgotten that he had once, during his period of transgression, tried to get close to her and she had rejected him decisively. But the sight of her now aroused his disgust so he turned to a prostitute, a second-rate singer at a nightclub called The Age of Youth, whom he had stayed in touch with, despite the fickleness of his love life. By that time she had given up work because she was too old, but she had not lost all her femininity. Before long they were married and had taken up residence in an elegant apartment in New Cairo. They performed the hajj together and lived in general peace and splendor. Wine had consumed Labib's liver and he began to suffer from internal bleeding while still head of the court of appeals. He was carried from Alexandria to his house in Cairo, where he died. He departed life when Egypt was at the height of its success a few months before the June defeat.

Lutfi Abd al-Azim Dawud

He was the first child of Abd al-Azim Dawud and Farida Husam. In terms of beauty, he was the image of his mother and his sister Fahima, while he owed his intellect to his father and grandfather. During childhood and adolescence, occasions for friendship with Amr's family, and Amer in particular, were firmly established, and he fell in love with the old quarter and

Radia's extraordinary eccentricity. He was enchanted by Matariya's beauty, just as she was by his good looks, and a modest romance developed in keeping with the customs of the day. Their hearts opened up expecting to meet a shower of happy tidings, but when Lutfi signaled his aspirations from afar, it was as if a bomb had exploded at the Dawud family villa on Sarayat Road. They forgot kinship, Amer and Iffat's love, and the fraternity between Amr and Abd al-Azim. They saw the gesture as a misguided lapse in taste and a route into the abyss. A barrier was placed around Lutfi until Matariya was engaged and the danger had disappeared. Radia was furious and rained her curses on those without roots. Amr felt pain in his heart and blood rushed to his face. Surur egged his brother on, "Your anger shouldn't be stifled."

However, Farida Husam's friendship supported Radia and, as usual, Amr was polite despite his agitation. Family ties triumphed over temporary upsets. How Dawud's daughters talked about Amr and Surur's daughters and vice versa! How atrociously Dawud's family joked about Ata's family and how cruelly Ata's ridiculed Dawud's! Nevertheless, solid foundations stood firm against the storms and hurricanes that raged over the great family. During those strange times, love's routine was forgotten. It was not long before Lutfi was busy with his medical studies and obtained his degree. He traveled to Germany as part of a delegation then returned to begin a career in research at the ministry of health. He demonstrated brilliance in both administration and learning and attained strong standing among the opposition parties despite his family's known affiliation. He was more independent than partisan and did not hesitate to pledge allegiance to the Crown as a loyal senior official. He was assigned the rank of bey, then pasha, while still between youth and middle age.

Amr played a historic role in Lutfi's marriage. He was a boyhood friend of a man who had been made president of the medical commission, Bahgat Bey Amr. He saw the Bey's daughter Amal, a graduate from La Mère de Dieu and a rare beauty, and, with his gentle heart and eagerness to please, had the idea of arranging a marriage between her and Lutfi. He became a kind emissary between Abd al-Azim's family and Bahgat's family and at his hands the happiest of marriages took place. The favor was appreciated by both families. A new family grew up in a villa in Dokki, an Egypto-European family, who frequently visited its progenitor, Amr Effendi, in his old house on Bayt al-Qadi Square. Amal was enchanted by the ancient quarter and Radia. Among the visitors of the grand houses of Ata, Dawud, and Baligh's families, she was a fresh rose that diffused a foreign fragrance and a new kind of magic that enchanted relatives and neighbors like the draw of Sufism. She gave birth to Farida, Mirfat, and Dawud, who moved abroad when they were older—Farida and Mirfat as the wives of two politicians, and Dawud as a doctor in Switzerland where he married a Swiss woman. Lutfi was among the few who were not affected by the afflictions of his class during the July Revolution and could retire as a minister. However, most of his savings, which were invested in shares and bonds, were lost with nationalization. He died of stomach cancer, not long after his father. He was in his seventies, which was considered young among Abd al-Azim's long-living family.

Mim

Mazin Ahmad Ata al-Murakibi

THE SWEETEST ROSE TO GLEAM in the Murakibi family mansion's large garden. The gentleness of his father, Ahmad Bey, and beauty of his mother, Fawziya Hanem, blossomed in him and he was one of those dearest to the families of Amr, Surur, and Dawud. Since childhood, he had loved his uncle's daughter Nadira, and she loved him too. Thus, he was the most miserable of all about the dispute that ripped the family apart, and thus, he was exposed to the fury of his brother, Adnan, the instigator of the trouble. He stumbled at school but decided nevertheless to take a degree in agriculture to prepare him for working life and to ensure that the same tragedy was not repeated. Though he was still quite young, he privately endeavored to secure Amr Effendi's blessing on his efforts to reconcile the angry brothers and secretly urged his beloved cousin to keep their love safe from the storm until it died down. When his amiable father fell sick with the illness that would kill him and the clouds of grief dispersed, his sadness over his father's death did not prevent him from wholeheartedly welcoming peace back into the family. At the time, he was in his final year of studies and resolved to announce his engagement once the year of mourning was over.

At the beginning of the following spring he traveled with a group of exchange students on a study trip to Alexandria. He decided to go for a swim with some friends in Shatby but was deceived by the waves and drowned. His death came as a violent blow to the family and in Nadira's heart it left a scar that would never heal. His possessions went to Adnan, who consequently became the richest man in Ata's family, though also the only one to whom the agriculture reform laws applied after the July Revolution.

Mahir Mahmud Ata al-Murakibi

He was born and grew up in the mansion on Khayrat Square. Like his brothers and sisters, his upbringing was serious and urbane. He was tall, slim, good looking, and palpably proud of his social status. He only visited his relatives on special occasions and avoided the Dawud family in particular. His school career was not promising so he made the war college the goal of his studies. He was infatuated with aristocratic life in all its manifestations, from a preference for the Crown over political parties to forging friendships within his class and exploiting his good looks to win the hearts of beautiful girls. He pestered his father with requests for money. Mahmud Bey wanted his sons to be brought up disciplined but not deprived and it troubled him that the boy would not fall in line. At the same time, he loved and admired him so pretended not to mind that his wife was biased toward him and granted his requests—old age and ill health having softened him by that time.

Mahir enrolled at the war college and graduated at the beginning of the Second World War. Through personal connections and his brother Abduh's influence, he joined the Free Officers Movement on the basis of superficial sentiments and without seriously believing what was said about the "people's suffering" and "class struggle." When the revolution came, he found himself among its intimates and leaped effortlessly to a rank his stunted academic achievements could never have brought him. He was uncomfortable with the agriculture reform laws, though they did not apply to anyone in the family but his cousin Adnan, but the scope of his ambition knew no ends. He rented an apartment in Zamalek for his romantic adventures. His star continued to rise and he was appointed to the leader's private guard. He stayed in his post after the Setback, up to Abdel Nasser's death. He was then pensioned off, so devoted himself to the apartment in Zamalek. All this time the idea of marriage never once crossed his mind. When presages of the infitah policy appeared, he was convinced by some friends to start dealing in imports. He sold his land and abandoned himself wholeheartedly to this new line of work and made a huge fortune. Abduh, Mahir, and Nadira were brought together in the mansion in their childlessness and effusion of wealth, which they believed they were amassing for others.

Mahmud Ata al-Murakibi

The first fruit of Ata al-Murakibi's marriage to the rich widow, Huda al-Alawzi, he was born, grew up, and matured in an atmosphere of glory and splendor in the mansion on Khayrat Square and the farm in Beni Suef. He knew nothing of his father's former life, but he mingled with his relatives—his sister Ni'ma, and her children, Rashwana, Amr, and Surur—from the beginning and his heart was saturated with love for the old quarter. The markings of a strong and proactive personality manifested at the outset, more apparent for their juxtaposition with the mild temper and gentle manners of his younger brother, Ahmad. Nevertheless, the two were equally unpromising in school and, like their cousins Amr and Surur, made do with the primary school certificate. Ahmad then settled into the life of privilege while Mahmud stuck with his father, an astute pupil, faithful follower, and hardy assistant.

He was a model of strength and coarseness; medium in

height, a hulking face, handsome features, and a large head supported by a short, thick neck. His demeanor, aggressive gaze, and solid frame bespoke challenge, struggle, and violence. His father found little occasion to censure him in his early teens other than a few flare-ups out in the fields, so arranged for him and his brother to marry two well-bred sisters from the neighboring Bakri family. Mahmud began a prosperous marriage with Nazli Hanem and his eyes never looked at another woman all his life. The partnership succeeded thanks to his attachment to the hanem and his wife's refinement and traditional dedication to her husband and marriage. As the days passed, she gave birth to Hasan, Shakira, Abduh, Nadira, and Mahir. From the very beginning, and with rare shrewdness, Mahmud was resolved on mastering his father's heart. He knew the man was tight-fisted so played the part of a miser in front of him, even though he was himself neither overly stingy nor free handed. At work, on the other hand, he won the man's admiration through his perseverance, precision, and judgment, as well as his excessive violence when dealing with others and his refusal to show leniency, as if it was a crime or betrayal. His father, for his part, suffered moments of cowardice and would say to him, "It's also not wise to make a new enemy every day."

"Everyone likes my brother, Ahmad, but I don't care who likes me. The only way to protect your rights is with force," the son replied.

Ata even exclaimed once, "I've got one son and two daughters!"

Mahmud was unconcerned by his abundant enemies and their rising numbers. He preferred to be feared rather than loved by either employees or business associates. The cases brought against him day to day and repeat visits to court with defense lawyers did not bother him. When his father, Ata, died and he was alone with his brother, Ahmad, and his mother, he said, "You're entitled to manage half of the estate."

Ahmad was confused. The bewilderment showed in his eyes.

"It's a struggle in a forest of wild beasts," Mahmud continued. "Nice people are lost there."

Ahmad was even more bewildered and confused. Mahmud said, "Would you agree to me managing the business alone?"

"Happily! You're my older brother and dear friend. We've only ever known love."

"And I've never neglected a religious duty in my life. I work as though God is watching me."

"I don't doubt it," said Ahmad and let out a deep, satisfied breath.

Thus, Mahmud took his father's place. It was a black day for the employees, watchmen, and business associates. He went about fields, farms, and the market like a steamroller, regarded with contempt, curses raining down on him from men and women alike. One night, returning to the mansion, a couple of anonymous men attacked him with clubs until he collapsed unconscious on the ground. They threw him in a ditch and disappeared into the darkness. Not long after, a patrol passed by and heard groaning from the ditch. They rushed over and rescued him from the brink of death. He was taken to hospital. When people heard the news they struck their foreheads in exasperation and cursed the bad luck that hastened to save him at the critical moment. He left hospital, healthy and recovered, with new contusions and scars from the surgery on his forehead, cheek, and neck, which made him look even grimmer and more ferocious. These did not, however, change his nature in any way, though he became better armed and more wary. His cousin Amr Effendi, the person closest to his heart, said to him, "My friend, you must adopt a different policy."

"People are made for one policy. Woe to he who backs away from it," Mahmud replied.

He would visit Bayt al-Qadi in his resplendent carriage, laden with gifts. He enjoyed chatting to Amr and Radia, then would become immersed in talking about his countless lawsuits. Once Amr said to him, laughing, "You'll soon be a legal expert like Abd al-Azim!"

He laughed—he often laughed in Bayt al-Qadi—and said, "I'd rather die than waive my rights."

"But this life isn't worth such toil," Radia burst out passionately.

"Dear dervish, we were created for toil," he guffawed.

He would visit Abd al-Azim Dawud in East Abbasiya, where he enjoyed sharing news of his success and affluence and discussed cases. When he had gone, Abd al-Azim would say to Farida, "Sickness is better than a meeting with that oaf."

"His wife is a precious jewel," Farida Hanem would say.

"Lord give her patience in her suffering!" Abd al-Azim would reply sarcastically.

Even Nazli Hanem, who loved him more than anything in the world, advised him to be more moderate. But nothing could divert him from his path, ever.

"Can't Abd al-Azim Dawud help you at all in your lawsuits?" she also asked.

"He affects probity to hide his depravity and lack of chivalry. He's an infidel and copycat of the English—he drinks whisky at lunch and supper!" he replied resentfully.

When the 1919 Revolution came, a new kind of emotion stirred in his heart for the first time. He was touched by the magic of its leader and donated several thousand Egyptian pounds to the cause. For the first time too he perceived in the simple peasants a frightening power he had not known before. When the different positions of the Crown, Adli, and the leader crystallized, he began to take stock of his accounts. He met with his brother at the mansion on Khayrat Square and asked him, "What are your thoughts on the current situation?"

"Sa'd is undoubtedly in the right," Ahmad said innocently.

"I'm asking what is in our best interest," he said coldly.

"I haven't thought about it," Ahmad said confused. "Do you think we should support Adli Pasha?"

"The Crown is the permanent center of power."

"You're always right, brother," Ahmad said simply.

"What is your social circle saying?"

"They are all for Sa'd."

"Publicize your political affiliation so as many people as possible know."

"Our nephews, Amr and Surur, support Sa'd too."

"They don't have anything at stake. The games are over. Don't imagine the English will leave Egypt. And don't imagine Egypt can survive without the English."

In return for pledging allegiance to the Crown, he and his brother were awarded the rank of bey. "Now the Dawud family must admit rank isn't restricted to them alone. . . ." he said to Ahmad. However, a revolution of another kind flared up in the family, this one led by his nephew Adnan. The family, both men and women, split into two rival factions. Opponents savored its misfortune while friends, like Amr and Rashwana, were sad. Even Surur said, "A curse has befallen that damned family."

They were not reunited until Ahmad's death, a few months after which Mahmud developed serious diabetes. Amr and Surur had passed away by this time and a melancholy compounded by the illness settled in Mahmud's heart. His determination flagged and he withdrew from the business. He spent most of his time in the mansion on Khayrat Square until a heart attack seized him one morning and he died. Nazli Hanem joined him two years later and Fawziya Hanem died in the same year. Only those destined for extra long life from that generation, like Radia, Abd al-Azim Pasha, and Baligh, remained; they were the ones whose lives stretched until the July Revolution.

Matariya Amr Aziz

She was born and grew up in Bayt al-Qadi, the third child of Amr and Radia. With her pretty face, slender figure, and amiability she most resembled Sadiqa, the aunt who committed suicide. She was also the most beautiful of the sisters, and quite possibly of all the girls in the family. Though she came into maturity in an atmosphere of religion and mysticism, she did not assimilate their underlying significance and believed that loving God and His messenger exempted her from religious duties. Her exquisite beauty stirred jealousy in her sisters' hearts, but as events unfolded this turned to pity. In her childhood and early teens, she was known for grace and mirth and for loving generously and being loved in return; not a woman or girl in Surur, Ata, or Abd al-Azim's families escaped her charm. Yet none of this could intercede on her behalf when her charm enticed a young man like Lutfi Abd al-Azim to contemplate marrying her, for charm too is limited by class consciousness. The first happy experience in her life thus became an emotional trial that immolated her tender heart and injured her pride. Her pain was slightly eased by the blaze of anger that flared up around her in her and her family's defense, as it was by the fact that she had not revealed her feelings. The battle thus turned on pride, then fell into the age-old chasm of tradition.

Not long after, a friend whom her mother had met at the tomb of Sidi Yahya ibn Uqab came with a proposal. Her mother regarded the location of their first meeting as a good omen and judged the woman, who lived not far away in the quarter of Watawit, to be a good person. The bridegroom—Muhammad Ibrahim—was a teacher at the Umm Ghulam School and in terms of diploma and profession was Amer's equal. Matariya saw him through the gap in the mashrabiya and was attracted to his wheat-colored face, plump body, and the pipe he smoked like the English. She was wedded to him in the house his mother owned in Watawit. Through good fortune, Matariya won her mother-in-law's heart, and enjoyed a bond of true love with her husband until the day he died. Year upon year radiated with happiness and harmony, and she gave birth to Ahmad, Shazli, and Amana—all three satellites of purity and grace. People were right to consider the house in Watawit among the happiest, in the true sense of the word. Muhammad Ibrahim was the second man to join Amr's family after Hamada al-Qinawi but he was urbane, gentle natured, cultured, and had a diverse library. His prim conversation and Hamada's chatter and groundless conceit could not have been more different. Muhammad found it impossible to genuinely make friends with Hamada but was very amiable with him in deference to Sadriya, whom he admired and whose virtues as a housewife had not escaped his notice. Those happy years would remain in Matariya's heart forever; the minutiae of daily life, the warmth of her husband's love, her mother-in-law's compassion and patience, the children with their bright promise. Then came the first blow of fate; Ahmad died in his fifth year. Matariya tasted the pain and profound sadness of a bereaved mother. Part of her throbbing heart, and the scent of her bereft spirit, began dwelling in the grave that spread in a swathe of new emotions before her tearful eyes. She loved Qasim all the more when she saw how inconsolable he was at the loss of her young son. She focused her wounded motherly love on Shazli and Amana, though her heart did not rejoice as she had hoped it would with their marriages. Her mother-in-law died in the 1930s, loading her with a burden to which she was not accustomed, and she mourned the death of her own father shortly before the Second World War and her uncle Surur's a few years later. She truly suffered for her strong attachment to her family. She regarded Shazli's marriage as a grave disappointment and considered it part of her bad luck.

"It's not as bad as you think," said Muhammad Ibrahim.

"He deserves a better bride," she complained.

"He knows best what makes him happy," said the man.

She followed Amana's success at school with satisfaction and hope. Then her beloved husband unexpectedly developed cirrhosis of the liver and was confined to his bed. His health deteriorated and he died in the summer holiday after Amana had passed the baccalaureate. Matariya met the harshest blow of fate yet and found herself a widow before fifty. Amana was forced to marry Abd al-Rahman Amin while Matariya stayed on in the house in Watawit with her maid, lonely and sad. Her worries were compounded by the troubles her daughter encountered in her marriage. She would console herself by visiting relatives—her mother, sisters, brothers, cousins, the families of Ata and Abd al-Azim, and, first and foremost, Shazli and Amana. She began to wither. Her features changed, though her unique quality—the love she gave and received from the family and people in general—remained. She was probably the only person in the family not to sever relations with her brother Hamid's wife, Shakira, after the couple separated in divorce. How she grieved over the premature deaths of Shazli's children! While Shazli's son, Muhammad, was still warding off his fate, she invoked God to preserve him for the sake of his father and herself, and entreated her mother, Radia, to shield him using whatever means. News of his martyrdom in the Tripartite Aggression came as the final blow. She withered even more.

It became clear she was suffering from cancer. Her health declined, going from bad to worse, until she died in her sixties. She was the first of the second generation in Amr's family, or rather the whole family, to pass away. Circumstances dictated that those closest to her did not mourn her as they might have; Shazli's sadness over his children did not leave much room for mourning, Radia was in her eighties and the grief of an octogenarian is short-lived, and Qasim lived in a neutral state of sadness and joy. Amana did not find anyone with whom to weep and strike her face in despair.

Mu'awiya al-Qalyubi

He was born and grew up in the house in Suq al-Zalat. His upbringing was purely religious and he took on his father's learning and manners even before they were together at al-Azhar. He displayed nobility and talent, with a particular fondness for grammar, which he taught at al-Azhar after obtaining his religious diploma. A few months before Mu'awiya's father died, he married his son to Galila al-Tarabishi, the daughter of Salman al-Tarabishi, who worked at a factory making tarbooshes for pashas. Mu'awiya took part in activities in the mosques around the quarter, which won his father-in-law's love and respect. Galila was taller than him, eccentric, high-strung, and full of popular superstitions. He was determined to teach her the true principles of her religion and a long but amicable struggle broke out between them. He gave to her and took from her. When he was sick he would surrender readily to her folk medicine. Her reputation spread around the quarter until it almost eclipsed his own. They were bound by love and, thanks to this, their marriage endured despite Galila's irascible nature and fanatical ideas. As the days passed, she gave birth to Radia, Shahira, Sadiqa, and Baligh.

When the Urabi Revolution came, the shaykh was full of enthusiasm. He was drawn to its current and supported it with heart and tongue. When it failed and the English occupied Egypt, he was one of many arrested and tried and was sentenced to five years in prison. Galila toured the tombs of saints invoking evil upon the khedive and the English. She managed the family with some money she had inherited from her father. Shaykh Mu'awiya left jail to find a changed world. No one remembered the revolution or any of its men, and if names were mentioned they were accompanied by curses. He found no sympathy except in the eyes of his old friend Yazid al-Misri, the watchman of Bayn al-Qasrayn's public fountain. He felt like an outsider. He was sad and kept to himself until he found a teaching post in a state school.

One day his friend Aziz said to him, "My son Amr works at the ministry of education. He's twenty and I want him to get married."

The shaykh grasped what Aziz was driving at and said, "By God's blessing."

"It's in your hands, with God's permission, and from your house," said Aziz.

"Radia my daughter and Amr my son!" said the shaykh.

Ni'ma Ata and her daughter, Rashwana, went to court Radia. They returned dazzled by Sadiqa's beauty and satisfied with Radia's good looks and lofty demeanor. Even so, Ni'ma asked, "Is she taller than Amr?"

"Not at all, mother. He's taller," said Rashwana reassuringly.

However, time overtook the shaykh before he could witness his daughter's wedding. The bridal hamper arrived by coincidence on the day he died, prompting Galila, with her individual interpretation of her heritage, to release a stream of ululation from the window then resume wailing for her dear deceased, which the quarter joked about for the rest of her life. The shaykh was buried in an enclosure nearby Aziz's own in the vicinity of Sidi Nagm al-Din.

Nun

Nadir Arif al-Minyawi

HE WAS BORN AND GREW UP IN DARB AL-AHMAR, the only son of Habiba Amr and Shaykh Arif al-Minyawi. He had no memory of his father but grew up in the abundant tender love of his mother and paternal grandmother. His grandmother died when he was six, but he found in the affection of Amr, Radia, and the rest of the family a way to forget he was a lonely orphan. It was perhaps fortunate that he yearned for success and was carried away by ambition from childhood. Yet he never appreciated the insane sacrifice his mother made on his behalf in refusing an excellent marriage proposal and remaining a widow for the rest of her life, after only two years married to his father.

Nadir grew into a handsome and fine young man and no period of his life was devoid of romantic adventures within his limited means. He obtained the baccalaureate in commerce during the First World War and found work in the Treasury. He despised his poverty and was always looking for a better future. To this end, he enrolled at an institute teaching English, mastered the art of typing, and put himself forward for an exam advertised by an English metal company. He was successful, so he quit the civil service to work for the company's accounts department. The move frightened his maternal aunts and uncles, cousins, and mother, but he said with a confidence unknown in the family, "There's no future in government employment."

His finances improved but his ambition was not sated. As an ambitious young man dreaming of fortune he was uncomfortable with the course of the July Revolution. His fears were realized after the Tripartite Aggression and the impounding of British companies, at which point he reluctantly found himself a civil servant once more. He studied the situation in his family and its branches in the light of the revolution's new reality. He found representatives of the revolution, like Abduh Mahmud, Mahir Mahmud, and his cousin Hakim, in the families of Ata al-Murakibi and Aunt Samira, and secretly made up his mind to marry either Abduh and Mahir's sister Nadira or Hakim's sister Hanuma. He consulted his mother, who said, "Hanuma's closer to us and prettier." At his suggestion she proposed to her on his behalf. Hanuma was a radio broadcaster with strong principles and a similar nature to her brother Salim. She had refused the hand of her cousin Aql, but agreed to marry Nadir. The wedding was held in an apartment on Hasan Sabri Street in Zamalek. Nadir urged his mother to come and live with him, but she refused to leave Darb al-Ahmar or move away from the blessed old quarter, where her dear mother and many of her sisters and uncle's daughters lived. The new family was blessed with happiness and Hanuma gave birth to three daughters, Samira, Radia, and Safa. Relations between Nadir and Hakim strengthened and, thanks to Hakim, Nadir was promoted to Head of Accounts. His salary increased beyond the dreams of his other civil servant relatives but his ambition knew no limits. With nationalization, he was appointed Chairman of Company Administration but still was not satisfied. "What more do you want?" Hanuma asked him.

"I don't like fixed salaries," he replied ambiguously.

"I don't mind wealth so long as it's combined with purity," Hanuma said with clarity.

He noticed a look of fear in her eyes and said quickly, "Of course."

He sensed the partner of his life was not partner to his ambition. He believed deep down that the only difference between people inside and outside jail was luck, not nature or principles, and that mankind was a wretched bunch from which only the shrewd and strong escaped. He regarded his wife as an extension of the foolish general attitudes he had to flatter if he wanted to realize his ambition. He began consolidating relations with certain officers and men in the private sector until June 5, when they were all exposed. He was satisfied to be simply pensioned off, again thanks to Hakim, but Hanuma raised a storm that culminated in divorce.

"You're only responsible for yourself," Samira assured Hanuma with her usual calm.

"But I can't just shut my eyes and destroy everything my life is built on," the young woman replied fiercely.

Hanuma kept the apartment and their daughters while Nadir began to live between hotels and Darb al-Ahmar, explaining the divorce to his innocent mother in terms of a disagreement that ruined the marriage. When the situation changed and the first indications of the infitah policy appeared he began to breathe once more. He derived from this unexpected situation a life he had never before dreamed of. He busied himself determinedly with imports and finally realized the dream he had entertained since childhood. The world spread out before him at home and abroad. On one of his journeys he met an Australian widow, married her, and moved in with her in a villa in al-Ma'adi. He would often laugh and say, "It's my rightful share; fortune is for the strong, morality for the weak."

Nadira Mahmud Ata al-Murakibi

She was the fourth child of Mahmud Bey Ata. She was born and grew up in the mansion on Khayrat Square in an environment steeped in splendor and comfort. She was nice looking but less so than her brothers. She was similar in nature, principles, and piety to her older sister, Shakira, and very compliant and gentle too. She had a sharp mind and loved school. Her father, having been conquered by current trends, did not object to her continuing her education. Her childhood happiness was crowned by the love that united her with her cousin Mazin. He was her knight in shining armor from adolescence until the day he died, or rather all her life. She loved him like nothing else in the world and pinned all her dreams, happiness, and hope on him. How she fretted over the quarrel that rent the family! How she feared its implications for her happiness and aspirations! "Papa is too angry," she said to her mother.

Their bond was not severed through the many years of dispute. Meanwhile, she passed the baccalaureate and enrolled at the faculty of medicine. Then came the disaster in which Mazin perished. He vanished from her world and she virtually went mad with grief, or rather anger. She spent a year in the mansion, prisoner to depression, then continued her studies with a hardened heart, set on renouncing the world. She emerged from that period with two bitter experiences: the death of her beloved and her sister's disappointing marriage. She applied all her energy to work, solitude, and religious readings. Good opportunities to marry came her way but she instinctively thought the worst and hated the idea of married life. She specialized in pediatric medicine, took a doctorate, and was more and more successful every day. She paid no attention to her brothers' advice to reconsider marriage and persisted with her work, solitude, and piety until the train left her behind, unapologetic, registered in the sad world as a unique, unrepeatable entity. Shakira, Abduh, Nadira, and Mahir assembled in the mansion in old age, as they had done at the start of their lives, living examples of success and failure.

Ni'ma Ata al-Murakibi

Ata al-Murakibi and Sakina Gal'ad al-Mughawiri's daughter, she was born and grew up in the house in al-Ghuriya. She inherited her mother's wide eyes and copious black hair together with good health, which her mother had not known. When Yazid al-Misri decided to arrange a marriage for his son Aziz, she fulfilled the criteria: chaste, beautiful, and the daughter of his neighbor and friend, Ata al-Murakibi. Ni'ma was wedded to Aziz and moved to a different floor of the same house in al-Ghuriya. She was a good example of a sensible, economizing, and obedient wife and gave birth to Rashwana, Amr, and Surur. Her father's marriage to the rich widow came as a shock. She watched bewildered as he climbed into a different class. She visited the new mansion on Khayrat Square and the farm in Beni Suef and was utterly dazzled by what she saw; she could not believe her eyes. She anticipated a shower of charity but was disappointed, for, with the exception of a few gifts on festivals, the man was tight-fisted, as though she were not his daughter or Mahmud and Ahmad's older sister. "He's a miser. He holds back his prosperity," said Aziz.

She defended her father despite some resentment, "No. He's just afraid the lady will accuse him of squandering her fortune!"

She was God-fearing but nevertheless hoped the widow would depart for the Hereafter before her father so she could inherit and bequeath some of the money to help Rashwana, Amr, and Surur in their lives. But the man died a short while before his wife, frustrating her hopes in death as he had in life. In the end, the fact that her two brothers, Mahmud and Ahmad, interacted with her and her children and were dutiful to them made her forget her sorrows. She reciprocated their love until the end of her life. She lived to delight in her grandchildren and departed the world two years after Aziz.

Nihad Hamada al-Qinawi

The first child of Sadriya and Hamada al-Qinawi, she was born and grew up in Khan Ga'far. She was cheerful in Bayt al-Qadi as a child and enjoyed special favor with Amr and Radia as the first grandchild. She was moderately pretty and received a small measure of education, which she soon forgot. When she was nearly fifteen, a middle-aged village mayor, a relative of her father, asked to marry her. Her father welcomed him enthusiastically and Sadriya realized with profound sorrow that she was to be separated from her daughter forevermore, that she would only see her on special occasions, and that from now on her daughter's roots would be in Upper Egypt.

Nihad acclimatized to her new surroundings, adopted new mannerisms, and took on a new dialect. She bore the village mayor ten children, half of them boys, the other half girls. Whenever she visited Cairo as a stranger, eyes would gaze at her curiously, for she was the picture of a typical village mayor's wife with her vast body and gold jewelry covering arms and neck. But she was the kind of stranger who provoked laughter.

Ha'

Hanuma Hussein Qabil

THE YOUNGEST DAUGHTER OF SAMIRA and Hussein Qabil, she
was born and grew up in the house on Ibn Khaldun Street. Her
beauty was like her mother's and she was tall, slim, and intelligent, had firmly held morals and principles, and was very similar to her younger brother, Salim. She excelled at school and
enrolled in the French language department of the faculty of
arts. She was enthusiastic about the July Revolution as a movement for reform and morality but changed her mind when it sentenced Salim to jail and did not hesitate to criticize Hakim for
supporting it. She graduated from college and went into radio,
thanks to her good results on the one hand, and Hakim's recom-
mendation on the other. Sadriya's son Aql wanted to marry her
but she rejected him on account of her height and his shortness.
"We would make a ridiculous sight walking down the street
together," she told her mother. She agreed to marry Nadir, for
he had a good job, was good looking, and she thought highly of
his morals. They lived their life together in an elegant apartment
on Hasan Sabri Street in Zamalek and she gave birth to Samira,
Radia, and Safa. When his deviation came to light, she raised a
violent storm, which Nadir had not expected from his life partner. She told him frankly, "I refuse to go on living with a man
who has clearly gone astray." Samira hated the idea of divorce

and tried to convince her that it was not her responsibility, that she must weigh up the consequences of her decision for her daughters. But she said to her mother, "He is diminished in my opinion and there's nothing I can do about it."

The dispute thus ended in divorce. Hanuma kept the daughters with her in the apartment in Zamalek and brought them up in her image without once regretting her harsh decision. The days went by and the time came for the girls to marry. However, rising costs and the problem of obtaining an apartment made marriage complicated. Nadir overcame all the difficulties by buying an apartment for each daughter and properly furnishing them. "He's their father and he's responsible for them," Hanuma said to console herself.

But she could not ignore the bitter truth that, were it not for his unlawful money, it would have been hard for any of the daughters to settle in a marital home. She asked herself with deep regret, Isn't it possible to lead a respectable life anymore?

Waw

Wahida Hamid Amr

THE FIRST CHILD OF HAMID AND SHAKIRA, she was born and grew up in the mansion on Khayrat Square and played through childhood in its vast lush garden. From childhood, it was clear she was intelligent, moderately pretty, and had a cheerful soul, which the winds of misfortune would destroy. From early life, melancholy permeated her heart amid the soured climate of her parents' marriage. She absorbed her mother's constant afflictions until an aversion to her father settled inside her. Her brother, Salih, offered no comfort with his bluntness and pursuit of people for their sins, as though he was their reckoner. Then came the split between her grandfather Mahmud and his brother, Ahmad, putting an end to her last remaining hope of a life with any optimism or happiness. She heard about her father's relatives' hostility toward her mother, their pointed comments, and the many tragedies that produced cracks in the branches of the family, until she subconsciously accepted that life was a stream of relentless sorrows, deviations, and agitations. Her only solace was in study, where she excelled. She enrolled at the faculty of medicine, like her aunt Nadira, and as soon as the opportunity to work in Saudi Arabia arose she emigrated. After years of absence, it came as a surprise to her mother to receive a letter informing her that she was marrying a Pakistani who worked at her hospital.

Warda Hamada al-Qinawi

She was the third child of Sadriya and Hamada. She was born and grew up in Khan Ga'far but loved dearly the old house in Bayt al-Qadi. She was devoted to her grandmother Radia, and her grandmother reciprocated her love.

"Warda is your most beautiful daughter but her mind is her most distinguishing feature," Radia would say to Sadriya.

She was engaged to a young cousin of her father before she had reached the legal age to marry but contracted malaria and was unable to fight it. She died, leaving a wound in her mother's heart that never healed.

Yazid al-Misri

HE ARRIVED IN CAIRO a few days before the French invasion. He came from a family of druggists in Alexandria, which was wiped out by an epidemic, every man and woman in it, leaving only himself. He detested the city, made up his mind to leave, and wended his way to Cairo. He had with him a little money and a rare quality in those days, namely the reading and writing skills he had learned at a religious institute before he was torn away to help his father at the drug store. He was lost in Cairo at first, then found lodgings in a house in al-Ghuriya and a job as a treasurer for a paper supplier. He was young and had a robust body, dark brown skin, and distinct features. He wore a gallabiya, cloak, and turban and, because of his piety and loneliness, his soul craved marriage. He noticed Farga al-Sayyad selling fish on the road and was attracted to her. With the help of his neighbor Ata al-Murakibi, he married her. She gave birth to many children, of whom Aziz and Dawud survived, and he lived to witness the birth of his grandchildren: Rashwana, Amr, and Surur. Sidi Nagm al-Din visited him in a dream and instructed him to build his grave near his tomb. He complied with the order, constructing an enclosure where he was buried and which, to this day, welcomes his deceased descendants from all over Cairo.

Glossary

1919 Revolution A series of demonstrations and uprisings across Egypt between March and April 1919 protesting the British Occupation, sparked by the arrest and exile of Sa'd Zaghloul and other Wafdists seeking Egyptian independence.

Adli Yakan Pasha (1846–1933) Prime minister of Egypt in the 1920s. Leader of the Liberal Party and political rival of Sa'd Zaghloul.

Anwar Sadat (1918–81) Third president of Egypt from 1970 until his assassination in 1981 by fundamentalists, following the Camp David Accords and peace agreement with Israel.

bey Title for Egyptian and Turkish dignitaries, ranked below pasha.

dervish Sufi or mystical figure, popularly regarded as a source of wisdom and enlightenment, often consulted for solutions to problems and cures.

effendi Title of respect or courtesy, generally applied to members of the learned professions and government officials.

Free Officers Movement Underground revolutionary group of young army officers founded by Gamal Abdel Nasser, which conducted the military coup of 1952.

gallabiya Simple-cut full-length garment, commonly worn by Egyptian peasants.

Gamal Abdel Nasser (1918–70) First Egyptian president, from 1956 to 1970. Charismatic leader and champion of Arab socialism and pan-Arabism.

hanem Title of respect for women of the aristocracy, similar to "lady."

infitah Open-door policy. The opening up of the Egyptian market to private investment under Sadat in the 1970s, ending the public sector's hold on Egypt's economy.

Ismail Sidqi (1875–1950) Prime Minister of Egypt from 1930 to 1933, unpopular for abolishing the 1923 Constitution.

July Revolution Military coup executed by the Free Officers Movement on July 23, 1952, which led to the abolishment of the Egyptian monarchy and declared Egypt a republic.

June 5 The first day of the Six Day War of 1967, when Israel launched a preemptive attack on Egypt with devastating consequences for the Egyptian air force and Arab morale generally.

mashrabiya Wooden oriel or projecting oriel window with a wooden latticework enclosure.

May 15 (1971) Sadat arrests a number of important men from the Nasser era and charges them with plotting a coup against the government.

Misr al-Fatah   Young Egypt Party. Political party founded in 1936 by Ahmed Hussein.

Muhammad Farid   (1868–1919) President of the Egyptian National Party from 1908 to 1919 after Mustafa Kamil, strong advocate of education and reform.

Muhammad Mahmud   (1877–1941) Twice prime minister of Egypt: in the 1920s under the British Mandate and in the 1930s after independence.

Mustafa al-Nahhas   (1879–1965) Leader of the Wafd Party from 1927 to 1952 and prime minister of Egypt a number of times from the 1920s to the 1950s.

Mustafa Kamil   (1874–1908) Journalist and Egyptian nationalist. Founder of the nationalist newspaper al-Liwa' in 1900 and the Egyptian National Party (Watani Party) in 1907.

narghile   Shisha; hookah. Water pipe with glass base over which tobacco is burned on coals and smoked through a pipe. Popular in cafés in Egypt.

Occupation, the   (1882–1952) The British Occupation of Egypt that began under Khedive Tawfiq. Egypt was granted independence in 1922, but Britain retained control of communications and defense until the 1952 revolution.

October 6   The date in 1973 on which Egyptian and Syrian troops crossed the ceasefire lines in the Sinai and Golan Heights, captured by Israel in 1967. The first day of the Yom Kippur War.

pasha   An honorary title awarded to Egyptians of high rank in the service of the Ottomans.

Sa'd Zaghloul (1859–1927) Leader of the Wafd party and nationalist movement of 1918–19. Key figure in the journey toward Egypt's independence. He was briefly prime minister in 1924.

September 1981 The month of Anwar Sadat's violent crackdown on Islamists and other opponents of his government, including journalists and intellectuals.

Setback, the Al-Naksa. The devastating defeat of Arab forces by the Israeli army in the Six-Day War of June 1967.

sidi Form of address used for men, equivalent to "mister."

Tripartite Aggression, the The Suez Crisis of 1956. Britain, France, and Israel launched a military attack on Egypt following the nationalization of the Suez Canal.

Umma Party Political party that advocated a gradual winning of independence through cooperation with Britain. Founded in 1907.

Urabi Revolution (1879–82) Important uprising against the Khedive and European influence in Egypt led by Colonel Ahmad Urabi.

Wafd Party The party of Sa'd Zaghloul and main Egyptian nationalist party in the first half of the twentieth century.

War of Attrition, the (1967–70) The state of war and hostility between Egypt and Israel from 1967 to 1970.

Watani Party Egyptian National Party, founded by Mustafa Kamil in 1907.

Translator's Note

MORNING AND EVENING TALK WAS WRITTEN in Naguib Mahfouz's last and most experimental phase of writing, at a time when he was particularly concerned with exploring new ways of expressing favorite themes—time, fate, politics, morality, the sources of evil, change—and taking the Arabic novel into new areas, like magical realism, folktale, and, on this occasion, biography. *Morning and Evening Talk* was also written when Mahfouz was an old man approaching his eightieth birthday and in a reflective mood. He had lived through some of the most exciting events in Egypt's modern history—the 1919 Revolution and struggle for independence, two world wars, the Free Officers Revolution in 1952, the Suez crisis, the Six-Day War, the October War of 1973 (the Yom Kippur War), the assassination of President Sadat—and it was only natural that in old age he should look back and wonder whether it had all been worth it. But the story of modern Egypt really began in 1798 when Napoleon's troops landed in Alexandria, so Mahfouz makes this the starting point of *Morning and Evening Talk*. The story begins at the turn of the nineteenth century—before the Urabi Revolution, Muhammad Ali's reforms, and the encounter with British and French colonialism transformed the face of Egyptian society and set it on the road to modernity—and ends sometime in the 1980s. As such the book represents an attempt by the author to come to terms with the events of the last two centuries.

Morning and Evening Talk is made up of sixty-seven character sketches from three Egyptian families—those of Yazid al-Misri, Ata al-Murakibi, and Shaykh al-Qalyubi—arranged alphabetically according to the name of the title character. The lexicographical arrangement of the text evokes the great Arab biographical dictionaries of the classical period, which record the lives of rulers, nobles, scholars, poets, and other important figures. However, Mahfouz peoples his novel with everyday Egyptians, reminding us of something the medieval Arab biographers apparently overlooked: that history is the sum total of people's lives; that the story of a nation is the story of its citizens as much as its leaders and remarkable men. The idea of *Morning and Evening Talk* is to bring together many individual narratives to tell the larger story of modern Egypt, almost like a jigsaw puzzle that the reader must piece together in order to understand events in their chronological context and logical sequence. The unusual structure of the novel also has another important purpose. The reader of *Morning and Evening Talk* finds symptoms of social breakdown everywhere in the text: as time goes by the father loses his authority, family ties grow weaker, and the family tree is increasingly dispersed across the city of Cairo and beyond. The narrative fragmentation of *Morning and Evening Talk* is thus an embodiment of the erosion of traditional Arab society, and the family nucleus in particular.

The novel opens with a tragic event, the death of a child, that in many ways sets the scene for what is to come. *Morning and Evening Talk* is a tale of endings and cruel twists of fate: children die before their parents; husbands perish, leaving families to struggle on meager means; and characters see their fortunes reversed overnight as their party or patron falls out of favor, or when war and other events over which they have no control appear out of nowhere. Yet the book is not without hope, for the corollary of sudden downfall is swift ascent—the July Revolution may be bad news for Halim, Hamid, and Hasan, but for Abduh, Mahir, and Hakim, it brings promotion and fortune, even if such things tend to be transitory in Mahfouz's world. Moreover, the eccentric person of Radia, and the friendship and humor that punctuate the narrative, are evidence enough that the indomitable spirit of Egypt lives on in the modern era, unscathed by all the change and upheaval.

Like many of Mahfouz's novels, *Morning and Evening Talk* is also a search. It is a journey through the homes, cafés, offices, and other haunts of the everyday Egyptian, watching and listening carefully in order to assess whether Egypt is better off now than it was back in 1798. It would be disingenuous to suggest there is a simple answer to such a question, and Mahfouz is certainly too wise to imply one. Instead he paints a vivid picture of Egypt over several generations and leaves readers to make up their own minds.

I would like to thank Feras Hamza, Philip Stewart, and Sabry Hafez for their invaluable help.

Christina Phillips

AKHENATEN
Dweller in Truth

The "heretic pharaoh," Akhenaten, who ruled Egypt during the 18th Dynasty (1540–1307 B.C.) was at once cruel and empathic, feminine and barbaric, mad and divinely inspired, eerily modern, and fascinatingly ethereal. In Mahfouz's novel, after the pharaoh's mysterious death, a young man questions Akhenaten's closest friends, his bitter enemies, and finally his enigmatic wife, Nefertiti, in an effort to discover what really happened in those dark days at Akhenaten's court.

Fiction/Literature/978-0-385-49909-5

ARABIAN NIGHTS AND DAYS

The Nobel Prize–winning novelist refashions the classic tales of Scheherazade in his own imaginative, spellbinding style. Here are genies and flying carpets, Aladdin and Sinbad, Ali Baba, and many other familiar stories made new by the magical pen of the acknowledged dean of Arabic letters.

Fiction/Literature/978-0-385-46901-2

THE BEGGAR, THE THIEF AND THE DOGS, AUTUMN QUAIL

In *The Beggar*, a man sacrifices his work and family to a series of illicit love affairs. Released from jail in post-Revolutionary times, the hero of *The Thief and the Dogs* blames an unjust society for his ill fortune, eventually bringing himself to destruction. *Autumn Quail* is a tale of political downfall about a corrupt bureaucrat who is one of the early victims of the purge after the 1952 revolution in Egypt.

Fiction/Literature/978-0-385-49835-7

THE DAY THE LEADER WAS KILLED

The time is 1981, Anwar al-Sadat is president, and Egypt is lurching into the modern world. *The Day the Leader Was Killed* relates the tale of a middle-class Cairene family. Rich with irony and infused with politics, the story is narrated alternately by the pious and mischievous family patriarch Muhtashimi Zayed, his hapless grandson Elwan, and Elwan's headstrong and beautiful fiancée, Randa.

Fiction/Literature/978-0-385-49922-4

ECHOES OF AN AUTOBIOGRAPHY

Here, in his first work of nonfiction to be published in the United States, Mahfouz considers the myriad perplexities of existence, including the preoccupation with old age and death and life's transitory nature. A departure from his bestselling and much-loved fiction, this unusual and thoughtful book is breathtaking evidence of the fact that Naguib Mahfouz is also a profound thinker of the first order.

Biography/Autobiography/978-0-385-48556-2

THE HARAFISH

The Harafish relates the tale of Ashur al-Nagi, a man who grows from humble beginnings to become a great leader. Generation after generation, however, Ashur's descendants grow further from his example. They lose touch with their origins as they amass and squander large fortunes, marry prostitutes, and develop deadly rivalries. The community's upper class has yet to encounter a threat from the legendary family, that is, until al-Nagi, like his noble ancestor, finds power among the Harafish, or the common people.

Fiction/Literature/978-0-385-42335-9

MIDAQ ALLEY

Midaq Alley centers around the residents of one of the hustling, teeming back alleys of Cairo. From Zaita the cripple-maker to Kirsha the café owner with a taste for young boys and drugs, to Abbas the barber who mistakes greed for love, to Hamida who sells her soul to escape the alley, these characters vividly evoke the sights, sounds, and smells of Cairo.

Fiction/Literature/978-0-385-26476-1

MIRAMAR

A highly charged, tightly written tale of intersecting lives, by the master of Middle Eastern fiction, *Miramar* provides an engaging and powerful story as well as a vivid portrait of the late 1960s. In the pension Miramar, a young girl hired to do chores for the residents provokes jealousies and conflicts that lead to violence and tragedy.

Fiction/Literature/978-0-385-26478-5